CAMPAIGNS AND CURSES

Other books in the
Weary Dragon Inn Series

Ale and Amnesia *(Newsletter Exclusive)*

Drinks and Sinkholes

Fiends and Festivals

Secrets and Snowflakes

Beasts and Baking

Magic and Molemen

Veils and Villains

Zealots and Zeniths

Campaigns and Curses

Perils and Potions

Royals and Ruses

CAMPAIGNS AND CURSES

Weary Dragon Inn

BOOK EIGHT

S. Usher Evans

Sun's Golden Ray Publishing
Pensacola, FL

Map created by Luke Beaber of Stardust Book Services
Line Editing by Danielle Fine, By Definition Editing

Sun's Golden Ray Publishing
Pensacola, FL
www.sgr-pub.com

For ordering information, please visit
www.sgr-pub.com/orders

Dedication

To Chris

On your 40th Birthday

You're old.

Town Hall
Witzel Butchery
Weary Dragon Inn
Library
Town Squ
Mackey Bakery

Pigsend Tea Shop
Flour Mill
Pigsend Village

Chapter One

Bev opened the back door to the Weary Dragon Inn, breathing in the cool morning air. While fall was still a few weeks off, there were tiny glimmers of relief from the sweltering temperatures that had gripped Pigsend since the start of summer. The solstice had been tough enough, what with magical storms and plots against the queen, but after the magic river had ebbed, things had gotten back to normal. Or, as normal as anything got in Pigsend.

The inn continued to do a steady business of overnight guests, which suited Bev fine. She'd gotten into the habit of suspecting anyone who wanted to stay more than a single night of being up to no good, warranted or not. Although it meant more laundry and tidying, it kept the chaos at a minimum to have people come and go daily.

She popped down to the root cellar to check on her bread dough. Since the start of the summer, she'd taken to making her rosemary bread the night before, letting it proof in the cooler space, and baking it sometime around midday. The dough hadn't risen as much as it usually did, but she left it down there anyway. The sun would be up soon enough, and with it, the temperatures and the dough would rise.

With the rest of her chores done, she tackled her kitchen with a wet rag and bucket. She liked to give it a good wipe down every few weeks, and it was looking a little dusty. She ran her rag over the canisters of flour, sugar, and salt, then along the shelf they sat on. As she worked, her trusty laelaps Biscuit, a golden-furred creature who looked more a dog than a magic-hunting menace, slept near the unlit hearth. Much like the overnight guests, Biscuit sleeping soundly meant nothing was amiss, and Bev was grateful for it.

But right as the clock struck seven, his small head perked up and his nose began twitching.

"Lillie's here, is she?" Bev asked with a chuckle. She tossed the rag into the dirty water, which she'd dump and refill as soon as she finished with Lillie, then headed to the front room.

Standing at Bev's front desk was Lillie Dean,

one of the two bakers from next door. She was in her mid-twenties, with coiled golden hair and freckles. Much like Biscuit's dog-like appearance hid his magical abilities, Lillie appeared to be human but was actually a pobyd, a creature with a preternatural ability to bake delicious things. This morning, she handed Bev a basket full of strawberry-and-cream tartlets.

"Getting fancy, are we?" Bev asked.

"Wanted to stretch my legs, so to speak," Lillie said with a smile. "Getting tired of muffins and pies and crumbles. Allen thought I was mad this morning, as I came in around three to get them going, but there's something so soothing about perfectly sliced strawberries on a bed of soft cream."

Bev took a bite, sighing with satisfaction. Although Lillie hadn't added any magic, they were still exquisite. "You aren't wrong. I could eat this whole basket." She pushed it to the side. "Better save them for the guests. They're in for a treat this morning."

"I've got to get back across the street. We've finally got enough of a break in the orders that we can start making jams for the winter. Goodness knows we've got plenty of fruit for it, and the weather's a little better for standing over a hot pot stirring. Allen's already got the first batch going."

"And how is...Allen?" Bev asked.

Lillie sighed. "The same. Unfortunately. We

really need to tell him."

During the solstice, Allen's latent pobyd magic, courtesy of his beloved mother, had suddenly appeared. He wasn't the only such person afflicted, as everyone in town with a hint of magic suddenly had more of it than they knew what to do with. But *unlike* everyone else in town, Allen's magic hadn't disappeared again.

It seemed he hadn't noticed, and Bev and Lillie hadn't told him. He'd so badly wanted to inherit his mother's magic, and to have it only temporarily might be worse than never having it at all. But the solstice had been weeks ago, and everything Allen made still held the lingering touch of pobyd magic.

"I know you don't want to break his heart," Lillie said. "But I can't let anything go out of the bakery without removing magic from it. Not to mention, if any soldier should pass through…"

"I know, I know. I was waiting to see if this magic would go away," Bev said. "I haven't heard from anyone else who's still feeling the effects. You aren't anymore, right?"

Lillie had been stuck in bed for days with a headache. "Not anymore, no. I stopped needing that iron tea the night after the solstice." She eyed Bev. "Any word from those herbologists?"

Bev shook her head. "They were smart enough to leave town, what with all the trouble they caused."

Two of Bev's guests had taken advantage of the full moon on the solstice to plant rare flowers in the dark forest. What they hadn't anticipated was those flowers infusing the underground magical river with such a surge in magic that it brought about a massive magical storm that threatened to destroy the town.

"I can't believe all that fuss was caused by something as simple as magic flowers," Lillie said. "A good thing Allen's father didn't find them."

"They're so rare. I don't think he knew what they were," Bev said.

Allen's father, Zed, was a high-ranking officer in the queen's army, and had been in town when all the chaos started. He was the unfortunate target of some mischief by a goblin drunk on magic.

"Did he ever figure out that Vellora's commander wasn't responsible for his bread-weapons and caterpillar-horses?" Lillie asked. "Or did he let things go because you turned him back from a gingerbread man?"

"The latter," Bev said. Hearing Lillie talk about it made the whole episode feel almost too unbelievable to be real. "I think there was a lot he let slide. Certainly let Andres leave without a fuss."

And a good thing, too. Andres had said he was in town to visit Vellora and talk to Bev about her past. But he'd revealed on the solstice that he was trying to gather like-minded people to his side to overthrow the queen. He'd asked Bev to join him, but she'd declined. She was, after all, a simple innkeeper.

Supposedly.

"I'm grateful we've had a few weeks of calm," Lillie said. "Before we know it, it'll be the Harvest Festival. And Wilda tells me there's a mayoral election happening between now and then, too."

"Yes, I've heard that." She wasn't looking forward to it. "Hendry's going to put her name in again, I reckon. Can't imagine what she'd do in town if she wasn't mayor."

"Do you think she has a shot?" Lillie asked. "I can't name one person who actually thinks she's doing a good job."

Bev shrugged. "I don't know how she keeps getting elected, unless she's spelling the whole town."

"That's certainly an explanation." Lillie wagged her brows. "Wilda's going to run."

"Really?" Wilda Murtagh was Lillie's housemate as well as a candlemaker. She also happened to be the cousin of the mayor of Middleburg, Miranda Twinsly, Mayor Hendry's nemesis.

"She's already gathering supporters," Lillie said. "Made me sign up first, of course. Said we're housemates and that supersedes all other loyalty."

"Hendry won't be happy, but what can you do?" Bev didn't care who won, but with a new mayor, she might be asked to solve the mysteries less often.

"Well, I've dilly-dallied long enough," Lillie said. "Have to get back to helping with the jam. But we really should tell Allen."

"I promise I'll tell him soon," Bev said.

She smiled. "In the meantime, I'll keep an eye on things. Who knows? Maybe today it'll finally disappear."

~

Bev wasn't hopeful about that, but she did appreciate that Lillie understood her hesitation. Allen had been so desperate for his mother's magic that he'd almost bartered away his entire livelihood to get it. The year before, Bev had caught him in conversation with a barus, a magical creature who could provide any flavor of magic in the form of a bauble. She'd helped him untangle himself from those bargains, and he'd gotten back on his feet and paid his debt to her five times over. Over the past year, his bakery business had grown by leaps and bounds. Of course, Lillie had helped, but Allen's hard work had laid the groundwork for success— without the use of his mother's magic.

"Tomorrow," Bev muttered to herself. "It's already too hot."

This morning's breeze was a far-off memory now. The sun was bearing down on the inn's roof, and the kitchen and front room were sweltering. Bev finished scrubbing the kitchen and had shaped her bread dough and put it back in the root cellar to delay the need to bake it a little longer. While down there, she'd checked her vegetable stores and found she could no longer put off going to the farmers' market.

But when she went to get her wagon, she heard an unfortunate *crack* and bent down to find one of her wheel spokes had broken.

"Well, isn't this fine," Bev muttered.

She went to the stable to retrieve some tools and pried off the wheel, inspecting it. The wood would have to be replaced and added to the iron axle, which meant a trip to the blacksmith's was in order. That presumably meant the farmers' market would have to wait, but as they were still trying to sell off all the magically-laced produce they'd grown during the solstice, she could head over there tomorrow.

With her broken wheel under her arm, Bev walked the length of the town to the blacksmith's shop. Gore Dewey, the smith, clearly didn't mind the heat as he banged a piece of white-hot metal with his mallet. When Bev walked into the forge, he stopped immediately and pulled off his helmet with a smile.

"Morning Bev," he said. "Wheel need fixing?"

"Indeed." Bev put it on the counter and smiled at him. "How are you, Gore?"

"Too busy," he said with a shake of his head. "And it's too quiet in here without Gilda around."

Bev nodded. Gore's apprentice Gilda had been offered her own forge and shop in the town of Silverkeep to the south. Lillie had been offered the same, but she'd politely declined for the moment, as she quite liked Pigsend and wasn't in a hurry to leave. Gilda, however, had jumped at the chance, as Gore hadn't shown any signs of retiring or giving her the shop.

"Have you heard from her?" Bev asked.

He nodded. "Got a letter from her saying she'd settled in and was busy gathering supplies. Those folks in Silverkeep were eager to get a blacksmith. Offered to pay for an entire forge full of equipment, too. But I sent her with a few things, if only to remind her where she came from."

He spoke of her fondly, with a little sadness, and Bev got the distinct impression Gore wasn't too happy about his apprentice leaving.

"Are you thinking about training someone else?" Bev asked, after a long pause.

"Bah." He made a face. "Put all my work into Gilda only to have her leave. Thought I might have some luck with her younger sister, but her parents put a stop to that. Not that I think Valta's got the chops to work the forge all summer long."

"I thought Valta was moving to Sheepsburg?" Bev asked. She was best friends with PJ Norris, and along with Grant Hamblin, had been planning to move closer to PJ's grandmother and Grant's sister

Vicky.

"Another thing her parents put a stop to," Gore said with a chuckle. "I hear she was real annoyed about it, too. But we can't have all the young folk leaving Pigsend. Who'll be left behind when the old folk can't work anymore?"

"There's still young Tallulah Painter," Bev said with a chuckle. The youngest member of the schoolhouse crowd wasn't even six yet.

Gore snorted. "Well, in any case, I've got my hands full. Freddie's putting his hat in the ring to run for mayor, and I've signed on to be his campaign manager."

"Really?" Bev frowned. Freddie and his husband Hans lived southeast of town and grew wheat and barley. "What does a farmer want to be mayor for?"

"Well, why wouldn't he?" Gore said with a frown. "We're a rural town, aren't we? Hendry's content to let the queen's folk do whatever they want. The farmers are suffering."

Bev hadn't heard anything about that. "Well, suppose that'll make for an interesting race," Bev said, hoping to keep her tone neutral. "Lillie tells me Wilda's entering, too."

"Wilda has no business running," Gore said with a shake of his head. "She's got too much Middleburg about her." He puffed out his chest. "No, Freddie is the obvious choice." He smiled at her. "I'm sure we can count on your support, eh,

Bev?"

Bev wasn't keen on offering *anyone* her support, at least not publicly, so she shook her head. "Still unsure. We've got several weeks, don't we?"

He made a face and adjusted his apron. "Well, I *do* hope I can count on you to keep quiet about what you saw in the forest, at least."

Bev started. "I'm sorry?"

"With Andres." He met her gaze unflinchingly. "You'll be kind enough not to mention it to anyone during the campaign, right? The people who know, know. The rest of the town doesn't need to hear about it."

"I've done my best to put that entire night out of my mind," Bev said with a smile. She'd even forgotten that Gore and Freddie were there. "It's not my business, and not something I want to think about."

"Good, I—" He shifted. "Ah, Mayor Hendry. Good afternoon."

Bev spun as Mayor Jo Hendry, pale-faced with silky black hair and bright red lips, sauntered into the forge. As usual, she didn't appear bothered by the heat, or anything else, nor did she seem surprised by Bev being in the shop.

"Hello, Gore, Bev," she said with her usual enigmatic smile. "I'm letting everyone in town know that the date for the Pigsend mayoral election has been moved up."

"To when?" Gore asked.

"Five days from now," she said, turning to leave. "Toodle-oo!"

Chapter Two

"Five days!" Gore exclaimed, but Hendry was already halfway down the street. "What in the world is she playing at?"

"Is it her decision to make?" Bev hadn't ever thought about the election, other than casting her vote a few years ago. "Shouldn't it be set by someone else? Like the queen or—?"

Gore snorted. "You'd think? That infernal woman dictates everything else."

Bev chuckled. "Well, suppose you should tell Freddie, if Hendry hasn't gotten to him yet. And good luck to the both of you."

Gore snorted, looking at Bev's wheel. "Might not be able to get to that today, then. Sorry, Bev. I might have a spare around here, though. Not sure it'll be exactly the same, but—"

"I can probably borrow Allen's wagon, or maybe the Witzels'," Bev said. "I'm sure you've got lots to do with the campaign." She patted the wheel. "Whenever you can get to it is fine."

He walked her out then headed south toward Freddie's farm. Why was a blacksmith so interested in the mayoral race?

"You'll be kind enough not to mention it to anyone during the campaign, right? The people who know, know. The rest of the town doesn't need to hear about it."

Bev had said she'd put Andres's meeting out of her mind, and she'd meant it, but she couldn't help but think that Freddie running was somehow connected. Still, it wasn't her business, and she didn't need to spend any more time thinking about it.

More curious was Hendry's sudden change of election date. Had the mayor heard that she was getting some competition and moved the election to throw them off? Bev wouldn't put it past her. Hendry was pretty ruthless when she wanted to be.

But when Bev opened the front door to the inn, she found the *actual* reason for the date change standing at her front desk, her tidy suitcase by her feet, and a large binder titled *Mayoral and Town Council Election Standards and Practices, Volume I* lying on the counter.

"Ms. Banks!" Bev exclaimed.

Petula Banks, the Harvest Festival judge, smiled at Bev with her thin-lipped, professional smile. "Ms. Bev. So good to see you again. I'm here to monitor the Pigsend mayoral election, and I require a room for the next week."

"O-oh," Bev said, hurrying to the front desk. "Well, sure. Very happy to have you back."

"I see you've still got that, erm, *dog*," Petula said, nodding to the laelaps.

Biscuit, who Bev had left behind to nap, watched Petula curiously, but didn't get up to sniff at her. Still, his tail wagged a little. Bev didn't have the heart to tell him he wasn't going to get to taste a spate of pies and bread for magic during this visit.

"I take it you're no longer judging festivals?" Bev asked.

"I've been promoted," Petula said, a little proudly. "Now working as an election monitor. Mostly small towns, still, but it's much more important work, you know. Her Majesty has no greater desire than ensuring that the local population has adequate representation."

Bev nodded, scribbling down Petula's name in the inn's guest book.

"I *do* hope this election will be free of the sorts of shenanigans we encountered during the Harvest Festival," Petula said with a knowing look.

"I don't have any other guests staying here masquerading as a judge," Bev said. "And though we've had quite the exciting summer, things have calmed down."

"Good. I want everything to be on the up-and-up for the next week." She opened the binder and pulled out a sheet of paper to read. "The next few days will be quite busy. Lots of election activities to get through."

"Really?" Bev chuckled. "Isn't it just…write a name down and put it in a hat? I think that's what we did the last election."

"My *dear* Bev," Petula said with a laugh. "How is anyone supposed to have faith in that? No, each of the candidates will have to submit themselves to a myriad of events, starting with this evening. The candidates and townsfolk will gather in the town hall for the official submission of candidate names. Those candidates will have to get signatures—"

"Signatures?" Bev asked.

"Well, yes," Petula said. "Each candidate will need a petition signed by no fewer than ten percent of the town population." She went back to her binder and flipped through the pages quickly. "I believe you're a town of one hundred fifty, are you not?"

Bev had no idea. "Sure."

"Fifteen signatures apiece then." She carefully replaced the paper she'd taken out. "After that, there's one night for candidates to set up their own rallies and campaign events. The next night, we'll have a question-and-answer session, where each of the candidates will make themselves available to talk with their constituents. The day before the election, we'll have a debate between the candidates. On election day, voting will begin promptly at four in the afternoon and run until midnight. At that point, I will count the votes and announce a winner."

"That certainly does sound busy," Bev said. "But is it enough time for the other candidates?"

"Whatever do you mean?"

"Hendry told us today the election's been moved up," Bev said. "Actually, just before I came back to the inn. I don't know if the other candidates know about all these events. As I said, the last election—"

"I wrote to Mayor Hendry weeks ago," Petula said with a frown. "Goodness, already off on the wrong foot, aren't we?" She picked up her suitcase. "Suppose I'd better get to it."

"To what?"

"Finding each of the prospective candidates and letting them know what's expected of them," Petula said. "I'm willing to delay the gathering of signatures until tomorrow, if that seems fairer. But goodness, what in the world was Mayor Hendry thinking, not telling people the election would be moved up?"

Bev knew *exactly* what Hendry was thinking but didn't voice it. "Would you like some help? I know of at least two people entering the race. I can head over to their houses and let them know."

Petula's face brightened. "Oh, that would be very helpful. Not that I—ahem—want to outsource my job, but I'm quite tired from the trip. I was hoping to grab a few moments' rest before I started my duties." She picked up her suitcase. "Please tell any potential candidates that we can delay the signature deadline a bit. In the interest of fairness. We'll cover all that in the event tonight."

"I'll set right out," Bev said with a nod. "Be back in a bit."

~

Wilda Murtagh was closest, so Bev headed there first. She lived three streets to the north, right down the block from Mayor Hendry in a quaint little cottage with pretty flowers out front. She'd rented her spare room to Lillie for the past few weeks.

When she knocked on the front door, Stella Brewer opened it. "Oh, hey, Bev! Come on in, we're getting going."

"Going?" Bev stepped inside and was struck by the flurry of activity happening in the small cottage.

Wilda was overseeing the painting of a banner proclaiming her candidacy and that it was *For Change!* Lillie was in the kitchen, carefully portioning out cookie dough, while telling Shasta,

Stella's twin, which paper she preferred to wrap the cookies in. Everything had a theme of lavender and yellow, which Bev took to be Wilda's campaign colors.

"Bev!" Wilda waved and walked over, looking brightly around. "Good afternoon. How in the world are you? Come to sign up for the campaign? Lillie's on my team."

Lillie looked up and waved, but then turned her attention back to the cookies and paper.

"Erm, no. The election—"

"Jo came by." Wilda rolled her eyes. "Trust that politician to do whatever possible to undercut the rest of us."

"Did she tell you it was moved up, or did she mention all the things you've got to do?" Bev asked.

"Like what?"

Bev laid out the different events, Wilda's face grew sourer. "No, the rat. She didn't mention any of that." She turned to those in the house and smiled. "I need at least fifteen signatures? I'm sure I can handle that by tonight." She puffed out her chest and strode over to a small desk in the corner, then found a spare piece of paper. "This should do, unless there's a specific format the submission has to be in."

"I'm really not sure," Bev said, rubbing the back of her neck. "But it is Petula, so—"

"Petula? *Banks?* From the Harvest Festival?"

Wilda spun around and her brows rose. "She's the election monitor?"

"Apparently," Bev said with a small shrug. "That's the reason for all the madness, I believe. And also why the election's been moved up. Petula's in town for the next week." Bev didn't want to volunteer that Petula had given Hendry notice about the changed date weeks ago, as there was already enough anger toward her.

"Well, I'll set to it now. Shasta? Maybe you can find some signatures for me. Get everyone in the room, for sure. Then start canvassing. I'm sure Freddie's got the farmer vote all sewn up, but we can find more folks in town who want someone with a bit more experience." She smiled at Bev again. "Will you be the first signature?"

Bev held up her hands. "I'm the messenger. Not sure I'm ready to put my name to anyone yet—"

"But why not?" Wilda asked. "Don't tell me you're going to vote for Hendry."

"After all she makes you do around town?" Shasta asked. "You're always the one having to solve problems. She never does anything to help you."

"That's true," Lillie offered from the kitchen.

"I haven't given it any thought," Bev said. "Not saying I'm not, erm, *Team Wilda*, but I need to think it over a bit. Not to mention, I've got to head to Freddie's and let him know what's going on. So..." She backed up. "Suppose I'll see everyone tonight."

Bev could feel Wilda's ire as she closed the door and headed south. It was true; Bev hadn't really thought about who she'd vote for. Hadn't given the election a second thought up until now, to be honest. She'd thought she'd cast her vote for Hendry, if only because she hadn't known there were other options. But while Wilda had been an excellent landlord to Lillie, Bev didn't know much about what she stood for.

"Suppose that's what the election events over the next week are for," Bev said.

Freddie and his husband Hans lived on a farm south of town, and it took Bev a bit to get there. But even before she walked up to the front steps, she could see activity in the front window. Like Wilda, Hendry had already told Freddie that he'd be up for election sooner than anticipated.

She rapped on the door, and Hans answered. The farmer was younger, with that sort of starry-eyed optimism that came with youth.

"Fred!" he called. "Bev's here!"

A chorus of cheers rose from the group, which was made up of even more people than had been at Wilda's. Freddie was in the corner, talking with Gore, and Dane Sterling was working on a banner of his own (though it was much less pretty than the one at Wilda's). Sonny Gray, the miller, was writing on flyers with three other farmers, and Eldred Nest, another farmer, was snoozing in the corner.

"Here to join the cause?" Hans asked excitedly.

"Just to pass on some information," Bev said, telling him about Petula's arrival and the election requirements. Hendry had once again left out key information about the process, and Bev couldn't quite shake the idea that she'd done it intentionally. Freddie didn't seem bothered by the fifteen-signature requirement, either, loudly proclaiming that he could get it sewn up by the official candidate submission this evening.

"Let's give Bev the honors first," Hans said, smiling at her. "Since she's the one who told us about it."

Once again, Bev had to demur, and once again, the opinion of everyone in the room shifted. No one could fathom that one might want to *think* about who to vote for.

"Suppose I'll see everyone else tonight," Bev said, inching toward the door. "Erm. Aside from you and Wilda and Hendry, do you know anyone else who's submitting their name? I'd like to give them a sporting heads up too."

Freddie shook his head. "Not that I know of. But Hendry would know better than us. Since she seems to know *everything*."

~

Bev headed back to town, making a beeline to

the town hall in the center of the village. The tall, white building had a clock in the tower, which reminded Bev she needed to get back to the inn to tend to any guests and start dinner. Petula had said the candidate submission would happen at six-thirty, which meant she'd have some hungry folks to feed.

But first, Bev wanted to have a word with Hendry. She'd realized, almost too late, that this should've been *Hendry*'s job, as the mayor had seen fit to at least tell her opponents that the date had moved. But not telling them anything else was grossly unfair, and Bev wanted to let her know.

Hendry was in her office, working quietly. It was a stark contrast to the furious activity happening at Wilda and Freddie's houses, and for the first time, Bev wondered if the ever-present mayor *might* lose her race. She didn't acknowledge Bev standing in her doorway, so Bev cleared her throat loudly.

"Yes, Bev, what can I do for you? Quite busy today."

"Well, I wanted to let you know Petula's at the inn—"

"Yes, already had a nice chat with her."

Bev started. "When?"

"She stopped here just an hour ago. I assume right before she headed to the inn."

Bev pursed her lips. "And she told you about all the events and the signatures and—"

"Mm. Yes. Had it done weeks ago."

Bev nodded. "And you didn't think to tell your opponents that?"

"Had no clue any of them were running until today," Hendry said with a sigh of exasperation. "Imagine my surprise. Wilda Murtagh of all people. She's got Middleburg all over her. If she thinks she's got a *shot*, she's dreaming." She turned the page. "And Freddie Silver? He's barely old enough to vote himself. Just wants to stretch his wings, I'm sure. Doubt he'll get more than the farmer vote. And a scant few that."

"You realize I had to walk around town and tell them about the signatures and campaign events," Bev said with pursed lips. "You didn't think it was pertinent, when you were telling them about the election date being moved up, to let them know all the requirements?"

Hendry didn't meet her gaze. "If they don't know how an election is run, Bev, it's *not* my fault. I'm the mayor. It's not my job to help my opponents."

Bev stared at her.

"Is there anything else? If not, I've got lots to do before the meeting tonight. So…"

Bev felt the urge to leave and turned to walk out before she knew what she was doing. She was on the front steps of the town hall when she came to and scowled at the building behind her.

That was perhaps how Hendry kept getting elected.

Zed Mackey had said he'd switched sides in the war because the magical people had an edge over everyone else, and it wasn't fair. Bev hadn't quite agreed with him, as the only people she knew who had magic used it to help others. But Hendry was content to use her empathetic powers to help *herself* and keep her job.

Would it be such a bad thing if Hendry lost? Would Freddie or Wilda be more eager to solve the town's problems instead of shoving them off on Bev?

"Suppose we'll find out." Bev was suddenly *very* interested in this evening's town hall, even if she wasn't ready to put her name to a candidate yet.

Chapter Three

With the town meeting in the evening, Bev moved dinner to five-thirty. Luckily, the usual diners —Etheldra Daws, Earl Dollman, Max Sterling, and Bardoff Boyd—had heard because they showed up a few minutes after Bev plated everything. Petula ate quickly then excused herself, saying she had lots to prepare before the townsfolk arrived at the hall. The others ate more slowly, talking about the election and who they might vote for.

"I don't have an opinion yet," Etheldra said, which surprised Bev, as the tea shop owner had an opinion about everything.

"Shasta and Stella are for Wilda," Bev said. "I would've thought—"

"What, do you think I let my employee tell me who I should vote for?" Etheldra snapped.

Bev simply picked at her food instead of reminding Etheldra that Shasta was supposedly a part-owner in the shop, and not an employee.

"I'm a bit on the fence, too," Earl said. "Freddie's nice enough, as is Wilda, but I need to know more about what they stand for."

"I'm for Freddie," Max said. "He's young. He's got some good ideas. I've offered to help with his campaign, too, but I couldn't get away from the library today."

"Well, I'm for Mayor Hendry," Bardoff said with a puff of his chest. "If there's one thing my trip to Queen's Capital taught me, it's that we need to stick with the people we know do the best job. Change is too risky these days."

"What else did you find out there?" Bev asked. The schoolteacher had gone to visit his old college and had returned the day before.

"Lots of talk about a potential attempt to overthrow the queen," Bardoff said, wiping his mouth with the napkin. "Ludicrous, if you ask me, but you know some people can't be content with peace."

"Overthrowing the queen?" Etheldra stared at him. "Didn't we settle that six years ago?"

Bardoff shrugged. "As I said, some people want to challenge the status quo. But for me, I'm happy with the lot we have. It's been a peaceful six years, and I'm in no hurry to overturn the apple cart."

Bev's gaze landed on Max, who was struggling to hide his true opinions. She'd been a little surprised the librarian hadn't been in the forest with Andres and the rest, as he'd always had kingside sympathies, especially as the queen's soldiers had ransacked his library and taken most of his magical books.

"Well, I don't think the Pigsend mayor race is going to cause that kind of trouble," Earl said, after a too-long pause. "But it might be nice to see someone else in charge. Goodness knows Hendry doesn't *do* anything around town, except lord over us all."

"Bev, who are you voting for?" Etheldra asked. "You've been awfully quiet."

"No clue," Bev said. "May not decide until the day of, you know? Lots to consider. I'm sure we'll find out more from the candidates in the next few days."

The clock neared six-thirty, and Bev took all the dishes to the kitchen to tackle later then followed the group to the town hall. Allen, Vellora, and Ida joined them, and when they arrived, the hall was already filled with people—more than the most contentious town meeting. Today, though, everyone was in good spirits, but there were clearly two distinct factions. Lavender and yellow banners hung from the left side, and Lillie, Shasta, Stella, and a few others had ribbons in their hair as they stood next to Wilda. Red and black, much more crudely drawn banners, decorated Freddie's side, which included Alice Estrich, Gore, Hans, Dane, and Eldred. It really was a battle of the farmers versus the city folk, though there were plenty more residents wandering around without any loyalty.

"Best of luck to everyone," Allen said, before heading over to Wilda's side.

"And to you," Vellora said with more than a little terseness, taking Ida's arm and all but dragging her over to Freddie's side.

"I hate elections," Earl said with a frown. "Look, there's a space over there."

He, Bev, and Etheldra bunched up in the small space, though Bev turned to watch the spectacle behind them. Or, more importantly, look for Hendry's faction.

"Seems the town is quite split," Bev said.

"We'll see who throws their name in," Etheldra said, settling in. "I have a feeling we haven't seen the true divisions yet."

"Got room for one more?" Pip Norris and his wife Holly stood in the aisle. They were the local farriers, kindhearted folk who'd been Earl's neighbors before he'd moved in with Etheldra. They also happened to be the parents of PJ Norris, who was a dragon shifter, but no one other than Bev knew that.

"Come on," Earl said, scooting closer to Etheldra, who made a face like she didn't think there was room for two more on the bench. "How are you, Pip? Holly?"

"Missing our boy," Holly said, a little tearfully. "We got another letter from him today. He's all settled in at Grant's apartment."

"Did Vicky get her inheritance sorted?" Bev asked.

Grant and his sister Vicky had found out they'd been left a large amount of money, though there was a stipulation that Vicky had to be married (and before her twenty-first birthday) before she was allowed to touch it. But Vicky's eldest aunt, who'd been unaware of the money *or* the stipulation, had promised to work with the bank to relax those requirements.

"And how," Holly said with a chuckle. "When we moved PJ in, their aunt Marion invited us to tea and regaled us with how she was able to—erm—convince the bank manager to give Vicky the funds now."

"I think it had more to do with the custodian of the account ending up in a queen's jail," Pip said darkly.

Bev nodded. Lucy, Vicky and Grant's other aunt, had been the one conspiring to keep the money from them, and had gone as far as to curse Vicky and Allen's wedding to keep her from it. Allen's soldier father had undone the curse and taken Lucy away.

"W-well, in any case, Vicky said she'd give Grant an income as long as he went to university, so he and PJ signed up for classes. Good timing, as they're about to begin again." She shook her head, spying Bardoff in the crowd. "I was hoping to find Mr. Boyd to tell him. He'll be overjoyed to hear it. Goodness knows he was always on the boys to be more than simple farmers."

"I'm sure you miss him, but I know being in Sheepsburg will be good for him," Bev said.

"Yes, if there's any mischief, there's more people to blame it on," Pip muttered.

Bev nodded. As long as PJ wore his amulet, his dragon shifter abilities were suppressed. And Bev didn't think Sheepsburg had the same temperamental magical river as Pigsend, either, so by all accounts, PJ should be quite safe in his new lodgings.

"It's sad not to see them around town," Bev said after a moment. "Perhaps selfishly, I was hoping he might take the inn from me one day."

"He did love you so," Holly said with a bright smile.

"As do we," Pip said with a nod.

"Hush now. It's starting," Etheldra barked.

Petula checked her timepiece and adjusted her shirt before striding to the front of the town hall with her large binder of rules and regulations in hand. The hum that had filled the space quieted, and all attention turned to the election monitor.

"Good evening, citizens of Pigsend," she said, her voice carrying across the space. She held herself like she was used to addressing crowds, and relished in everyone's attention. "My name is Petula Banks. Some of you may remember me as a judge from the Pigsend Harvest Festival last year."

She paused, perhaps hoping for applause or cheers, but when no one said anything, she continued.

"I have returned to your wonderful city to oversee the mayoral election. It's come to my attention that perhaps the news was not shared as *widely* as I'd hoped, but it appears everyone's gotten the message. I'm very grateful for the town's help in keeping the information flowing. Specifically, Bev, for assisting me earlier today."

Bev shifted in her seat as every gaze came to land on her. She'd hoped she could come to the town hall and avoid being the center of attention just once.

"In any case, I understand our candidates are ready, so we'll proceed with the first campaign event." She patted the thick book. "If anyone needs to review the official schedule of events, they can find it in my binder. Tonight, we will have the official declaration of candidates and submission of signatures. So, may I have the first candidate?"

Wilda stood, but in a flash, Hendry appeared in the doorway of her office. She wore a tunic of bright purple—which Bev recognized as tanddaes wool—and sashayed up the center aisle with a smile on her face. She produced a list from her pocket and handed it to Petula with a flourish.

"Jo Hendry," she said, her voice echoing across the crowd. "With twenty-three signatures."

Bev looked around. To her eye, no one looked pleased to see the mayor standing there.

Wilda rose with a disgruntled look on her face, her hands on her hips. "How do we know those signatures are real people? I've asked all over town, and *no one* wants Hendry back in office."

"You can check them yourself," Hendry replied coolly.

Wilda rose and marched over, all but snatching the list from Petula and scanning the names. "Some of these people don't even *live* in Pigsend. I don't even know who Marmet Pilando is."

"He lives half an hour from here," Ida said. "He's a pig farmer. But is he considered a Pigsend resident?"

Vellora smiled, as did Freddie.

"The town charter states that any person who lives between the cities of Middleburg, Centerville,

and Great Deerfield may vote in the local election,"
Hendry said with a lift of her shoulder. "Unlike
certain people, my attention is on *everyone* in my
jurisdiction, not only those I see daily."

Wilda's nostrils flared.

"Mayor Hendry is correct," Petula said. "I
reviewed the town charter in advance of the
election, as well, and am familiar with who can and
cannot cast their vote. I will be sure to check each
signature this evening to ensure they meet the
criteria, as well as anyone else who will be
submitting their name."

"Everyone on *my* list is here now, all *twenty-four*
of them," Wilda said, handing over her paper. "You
can name them, and they'll stand if you like. Might
make your job a little easier."

"That's quite all right," Petula said. "I'll be sure
to put your list through the same level of scrutiny."
She cleared her throat. "Are these our only two
candidates?"

"No!" The roar from Freddie's faction was loud
and immediate, and they applauded as Freddie rose
and walked the length of the hall. He had a satisfied
smile on his face as he handed Petula his list and
bowed.

"I have nearly thirty signatures," Freddie said
with a look at Hendry and Wilda. "And every one
of mine is here, too."

"Fifteen was the requisite amount," Petula said,

looking between them. "I do hope we'll have a fair, clean election. No funny business."

"Too late for that," Wilda said, glaring at Hendry. "As our *mayor* has already declared she's going to do whatever it takes to prevent anyone from taking her job."

"Yeah, what's the big idea, not telling us about the signatures?" Freddie snapped. "Not fair at all."

"Clearly, you were able to overcome the obstacle," Hendry said. "Part of being the mayor is being able to think on your feet and move quickly. How wonderful that you were able to demonstrate that ability to your supporters."

Freddie and Wilda stared at her, and Bev had to stifle a laugh. Hendry did have a way of twisting the truth in such a way that it made one wonder what reality was.

"W-well. It seems we're all on the same footing now," Petula said. "And we will be, now that I'm in town. I—"

"Excuse me?"

Bev jumped; the voice came from right next to her. Pip rose, his hat in his hands, and swallowed nervously. He stood for a moment, almost frozen, before Holly touched him gently and he jumped to attention.

"I'd like to throw my hat in the ring, if it's not too late," he said.

"Come on up," Petula said, a little too gently, as

if she pitied the man already.

There wasn't a sound as he walked to the front and faced Petula and the three candidates with a quiet solemnity. Bev hadn't ever considered him as a candidate for anything other than shoeing horses and other livestock. What cause would he have to run for mayor?

"I didn't know anything about these signatures or anything like that," Pip said, scratching the back of his neck. "Didn't even know the election had moved until…"

Petula nodded. "Yes, I was worried we missed someone. You have until noon tomorrow to—"

"That's not fair!" Freddie exclaimed. "We only had a few hours to get our signatures."

"If Pip can't get his here today, he shouldn't be allowed to run," Wilda said.

Hendry lifted a shoulder. "I say we give him a chance." The look on her face said she didn't think he actually *had* a chance of winning, but she approached the crowd, who were murmuring amongst themselves. "If anyone would like to stand and voice their support for Pip—"

"I would!" Earl rose quickly and raised his hand.

"Me, too!" Alice Estrich called out, much to the annoyance of Gore.

"And me!"

"Me, too!"

All over the town hall, hands rose and voices

called out in support of Pip. And within minutes, thirty-one people had signed a haphazard petition, including more than a few from the Freddie or Wilda side. Pip stared at the crowd, amazed and a little misty-eyed, before he turned to Petula with a satisfied smile.

"Here's my petition."

"Very good," Petula said. "Anyone else?"

No one stood, and Bev watched the four candidates. Wilda and Freddie's confidence had evaporated. Only Hendry didn't look annoyed by his sudden inclusion. She surveyed the crowd like she had the election in the bag already.

"Right." Petula put down the large binder and shook out her arms as if they were tired from carrying it. "Pigsend, here are your four candidates for mayor."

There was a smattering of applause, most fervently from those who'd stood and put their name in for Pip.

"Now, there will be a complete schedule available to anyone who wants it," Petula said. "It's imperative the citizens of Pigsend hear each of your viewpoints and platforms and make their decisions accordingly." She turned to the candidates. "Do you understand?"

They nodded, though Hendry waited until everyone else had before she dipped her head with a flourish.

"Yes, I think that covers it," Wilda said, checking the page on her large book. "Thank you so much for your participation this evening. I look forward to crowning our new mayor in the coming days."

Chapter Four

As soon as Petula closed the session, everyone rose and swarmed Pip. The other candidates escaped to their own factions, talking furiously with each other and casting nasty looks. Bev followed Etheldra as they joined Earl and the rest congratulating Pip. Holly looked overjoyed, tears streaming down her cheeks as pride shone on her face.

"What a surprise!" Earl said, clapping Pip on the back. "My friend Pip, running for mayor!"

"What made you do it?" Alice asked.

"Well, I think there's a lot that could be changed around here," Pip said. "Lots of folks who could be treated better, some better relationships we could have with our neighboring towns. No reason for us to only be the ones who get the short end of the stick."

On and on he went, and as he spoke, the crowd nodded. Even those who hadn't immediately voiced their support for him seemed on the verge of being convinced, and more gathered around him.

"I believe we're having our stump speeches next week," Hendry said, her voice echoing through the space.

Pip stopped and turned to her, a bashful look on his face. "Erm. Good luck to you, Jo."

"Until I've been kicked out of office, you may refer to me as *Mayor Hendry*," she said with a quirked brow. "But I daresay you have your work cut out for you. Can't imagine you've got anything planned or prepared for the grueling election season."

"It's five days," Etheldra said with a glare. "And he's not prepared or planned because *someone* withheld information from him and everyone else."

"It's all right," Pip said. "As you said, a mayor has to think on their feet. I'm sure we can figure something out."

"I'll be your campaign manager," Earl proclaimed, earning an eye roll from Etheldra.

"Just because we're married doesn't mean I'm going to vote for who you support," she snapped at him.

"Well, I hope I can earn your vote some other

way," Pip said.

He turned as more questions came at him, and Bev took that moment to peel away. As she surveyed the room, she counted the crowds near Wilda and Freddie, both sizable, but not nearly the size of Pip's.

But Hendry stood off to the side, surrounded by no one and scowling at the crowd as if they'd all personally offended her. Bev, for all her annoyance toward Hendry in the past, felt bad and walked up to her.

"How are you feeling about all this?" Bev asked.

"Just fine, Bev, dear." She tossed a raven lock over her shoulder. "You know these elections always have a way of working themselves out. People like a good story, but once they really stop to think about it, they'll make the right choice." She gestured to the two factions on the other side of the room. "These two amateurs talk nicely, but when push comes to shove, they're going to find themselves wanting. People may not *like* what I do, but they know I'm the best person for the job. That's the blessing and curse of being a politician."

Bev eyed her. "Do they, though?"

"Do they what?"

"Think you're the best person for the job?"

"Well, if they don't, they will." Hendry turned on her heel and all but floated out of the room.

Bev watched her go, once again noticing the

distinct purple hue of her tunic. Bev certainly hadn't *felt* befuddled or magicked during the session, but that didn't mean Hendry wouldn't spell everyone who walked into the voting booth to write her name in.

"If she wins without subterfuge, I'll eat my hat," Etheldra said with a glower. "Mark my words. We haven't seen the last of the campaign hijinks."

~

The next morning, Bev awoke and did her chores, once again enjoying the early morning coolness. It was downright pleasant, in fact, and she took her time mucking Sin's stall and tending to her herb garden. But the front door to the inn opened, so she crossed through the kitchen to find Allen with a basket of breakfast pastries.

"Morning," she said, inspecting the basket. "Lillie wanted to be fancy again?"

"I made these, actually," he said. "The ones Lillie made yesterday were so good, I wanted to try my hand. You know, in case Lillie decides she's tired of Pigsend and wants to leave. Try one."

Bev picked up a custard-filled spiral and took a bite. There was definitely pobyd magic in it, but it wasn't very obvious. She'd be fine serving them to Petula and the farmers who'd decided to stay the night after the town meeting, but she wouldn't serve them to a soldier.

"Has Lillie been in yet?" Bev asked lightly.

"Oh, don't tell me they're awful," Allen said, his face falling.

"No, no, they're scrumptious," Bev's cheeks warmed. "Perfectly delicious, actually." *Is it time to tell him?* "Are you two busy today?"

"Overwhelmed," he said. "We got the blueberry jam together yesterday, but once Wilda found out the election's this week, she told us to clear our schedule. Today, I've got to bake a hundred cookies to hand out. Lillie's back at the shop handling the orders we already had."

Bev was almost relieved. Not the time to tell him, then. "Wilda's certainly jumped into action, hasn't she?"

Allen nodded. "She was hopping mad last night that Hendry had got a list of farmers who barely make the cut. Says it's *unfair*."

"Well, I suppose Hendry does have an advantage, seeing as she's the current mayor," Bev said with a laugh. "But she's not endearing herself to potential voters with her underhanded tactics, I'll tell you that."

"You said it." He sighed. "But while Wilda's gold is nice, I was looking forward to a few days without much to do. Suppose we'll get it after the election."

"Suppose so." Bev beamed. "Good luck today."

Allen left, but he wasn't gone two minutes before the front door opened again, and Max came in with a thick book and tired smile.

"Morning, Max," Bev said, a little surprised. "What are you doing here so early?"

"Ms. Banks asked me to bring the list of all the people in town, so we might certify the name and address of everyone who signed a candidate petition yesterday," he said, placing the book on the table with a *thump* before taking a handkerchief and wiping his brow. "Tedious work, to be sure, but she insists it's necessary."

"Well, have a pastry while you wait," Bev said, bringing the basket over to him. "Allen brought them by."

"Ooh. I never let myself have any in Etheldra's shop, but I always want one." He twinkled his fingers above the basket for a moment before picking up one with a single strawberry slice laid inside. With a sigh, he took a bite and blinked happily. "Yes, perhaps a good thing I don't visit often. I could eat that whole basket."

"Please help yourself to as many as you like," Bev said with a smile.

"Just the one. They're too tempting." He made a dramatic face. "Take that basket away from me before I eat them all!"

Bev laughed and put it back on the counter. "Some event last night, hm? Who are you throwing your name in for, again? Freddie?"

He nodded. "Quite surprising of Pip to stand

up. If Freddie wasn't in, I might vote for him. He's got a good, grounded air about him. Wouldn't get caught up in all the power struggles Hendry seems to. And he'd be fair."

Bev wanted to ask Max if his support of Freddie had anything to do with Freddie's support of Andres, but before she could, Petula swept down the stairs. Today, she wore a crisp tunic with a securely attached pin boasting her position as the official election monitor. She carried her rules and regulations under her arm and greeted Max with a firm handshake.

"So good of you to come. We've got our work cut out for us this morning."

"Have a pastry," Bev said. "For energy."

Petula declined, for the moment, and settled in. Her first list was Hendry's, and as she called out a name, Max opened his own book and scoured it. His book had each person listed by last name, but not alphabetized within the letter, so it took him a minute to find each person.

It was tedious work, and Bev didn't think it a wise use of time to loiter and listen to them go through the hundred or so names, so she disappeared into the kitchen to continue her chores. She still had a few dishes from the night before to tackle, so she did those first then decided she might dust all the rugs in the inn, as it had been a few weeks since she'd done that.

But before she could drag the first one outside, the back door opened, and Hendry breezed in.

"Morning, Bev, dear." The mayor walked right to the kitchen door and peered through. "Ah, I see Petula's confirming our signatures."

"Yours seem to have passed muster," Bev said, walking to the hearth and rolling up the rug Biscuit usually slept on. It was absolutely filthy, covered in yellow fur, and Bev glared at the laelaps, who smiled back with a wag of his tail.

"Of course I did, Bev. This isn't my first election." She let out a haughty laugh. "That being said, there seems to be a *bit* more competition than usual, so I must pull out all the stops. I'd like to rent the inn for a campaign event tonight."

"You would?" Bev hadn't ever hosted such a thing. "What do you need?"

"Just the inn, and whatever you want to serve for dinner. I'll take care of payment to the butchers, and obviously, offer you a few gold for your trouble."

A few meant twenty gold coins, and Bev's brows shot up as she looked inside the bag Hendry handed her. "I don't need that much—"

"Take it, dear, as I know you have plenty to keep up with." She let out another high laugh, and Bev thought it rich that she *now* cared about Bev's workload after months of Bev having to clean up Pigsend's messes. "In any case, I would ask that you bake me something sweet. Perhaps a cherry pie? We could call it a Victory Cherry Pie."

Bev cleared her throat. "Shouldn't you be making this request of the bakers next door?"

"Those two are too deep in my opponent's pocket," Hendry said with a scowl. "Couldn't trust them not to poison the filling."

"Hendry," Bev said with a shake of her head. "Allen and Lillie wouldn't poison you."

"Wouldn't they? I don't trust their judgment, throwing their lot in with Wilda as they are." She adjusted her tunic. "I know you're capable. That crumble was delicious, if you ignored the willow bark and iron infusion."

Bev put her hands on her hips. The crumble she had made was intended to help with the excess magic floating around. And everyone who'd eaten it who *had* magic had complained it was acrid.

"In any case, you've been paid well enough that I'm sure you can steal a recipe or two from the bakers," she said with a flourish.

"I suppose I'll have to tell the regulars the inn is closed tonight," Bev said.

"Why would you do that?" Hendry replied with a laugh. "I expect a full house, so don't you dare tell anyone what I'm plotting, mmkay?"

"But—"

"Ta-ta, Bev. Lots to do today!"

With that, she was gone.

Bev *really* didn't want to host Hendry, nor did it feel right not to give her regulars a heads-up, especially as several were voting for other candidates, but gold was gold, and she'd be making dinner regardless. She'd plan to make a bit more.

She went out to her root cellar to take inventory, and remembered with a sigh that she still had a broken wagon wheel, and she doubted Gore had had time to fix it.

But as she was walking out of the cellar, the blacksmith himself strode into the backyard, wheel in hand.

"Morning, Bev!" he said, a little too brightly. "Thought I'd bring this by and get you all set up. I'm sure you need your wagon."

"Oh?" Bev tried to sound neutral. "Why's that?"

"Well, Freddie would like to rent the inn for a campaign event tonight," Gore said, walking over to the broken wagon and sitting down. He'd come prepared with some tools and set to putting the wheel on as he spoke. "Lots of folks hold you in high esteem, you know. It would mean the world to us if we could get the Weary Dragon's stamp of approval."

"Hiring me doesn't mean you've got my approval," Bev said, hoping Hendry wasn't spreading a false rumor around town. "Unfortunately, the inn is already booked for tonight. What about tomorrow?"

"The rest of the evenings until the election are spoken for," Gore said with a frown. "Tomorrow night's the question-and-answer session, then the debates, then the election. The only free evening is tonight."

"I could fit you in sometime in the afternoon, perhaps?" Bev said.

"Are you sure I can't convince you to cancel the reservation?" Gore said with a hopeful look. "I—"

"Bev, *dear*!" Wilda breezed into the backyard with a crate of produce in her arms, but her expression darkened when she spotted Gore. "Morning, Gore. Surprised to see you here."

"I've got business," he said, nodding to the wagon. "Bev's wagon was broken, and—"

"Yes, I *heard*." She adjusted the crate in her arms. "I thought I'd save you the trip and bring you a crate of produce. Allen told me about your wagon —such a shame! You're a busy woman, not a whole lot of time to be headed out to the market."

"Let me guess," Bev drawled with a smile. "You'd like to rent the inn for a campaign event?"

Her smile twitched, only a little. "Tonight?"

"Already tried," Gore said, as he rose with the wheel in hand. Bev frowned—was he not going to put it on since she declined him? "Apparently, it's already booked."

"By whom?" Wilda demanded with a sneer.

"Pip? How does he have enough gold?"

"Can't be Pip. I doubt he even knows what a campaign event is," Gore snapped. "It's probably Hendry. I thought I heard her slithering around a few minutes before I arrived." He reached into his pocket. "How much is she offering? I'll double it."

"I'll triple it," Wilda said with a haughty look. "After all, Bev, you don't want the Weary Dragon associated with such a *losing* campaign. If she has to scour the outer reaches of Pigsend to find people to support her, I daresay she's probably not going to win many votes. What are the chances those farmers even come into town to vote?"

"I *hate* to agree with Wilda," Gore said. "But you really should think about which campaign has the best look about it."

Bev glared at them. "Hosting a campaign is a business decision, which has no bearing on who I, personally, am going to vote for. And I have to say that as underhanded as Hendry was last night, what with not telling you folks what to expect, you two aren't acting any better right now, and I *know* that's not in your character." She put her hands on her hips. "So, while I appreciate the offers, tonight's already been booked. I'm happy to host any other time."

~

Wilda and Gore both declined Bev's suggestion, muttering to themselves and perhaps plotting Bev's demise. Wilda took the crate of produce with her, and Gore took the wheel back with him. Bev felt very strongly that an election was something that needed to be taken seriously, and bribes and favors weren't her style. Hendry had come to the inn first, so she got the booking.

As her wagon was still broken, she'd have to go by foot to get the cherries for Hendry's pie, as well as a sack of potatoes and other vegetables. Or ask the bakers or the Witzels for theirs. She hoped neither would be as sore as Gore and Wilda had been. It really left a bad taste in her mouth, especially with all Bev had done for this town...

...which led her to think about Pip, and his candidacy. There would be a mayor who'd truly be selfless and work for the greater good of the town. As much as she didn't want to make a decision yet, she did find herself wanting to declare for Pip.

At least, she thought so until she found him standing in her kitchen. Unlike the others, though, he had a piece of paper in his hand and his face was ashen gray.

"Pip?" Bev said. "What is it?"

"Someone delivered this letter early this morning," he said, handing it over.

I know your son is a dragon. Drop out of the race or else.

Chapter Five

"Not here," Bev said, looking through the door to the front room, where Max and Petula were still working through the list. "The root cellar."

Pip followed without a word. Bev replayed every conversation she'd had about PJ over the past few months, and parsed through every word she could recall. She'd been *very* careful never to mention PJ's abilities to anyone, though she had told Lillie there was a shifter in town. As far as the rest of the town was concerned, PJ and his friends had been suspected only as troublemaking teens, but when the disasters stopped, so did the curiosity. After it all ended, the most common refrain was that a trio of kindly old ladies had been the culprits (they were also dragon shifters, but they were trying to undo the damage PJ was unknowingly causing), as their departure had coincided with the last chaotic event.

Bev was happy to let people think that, as PJ was perfectly safe while he wore the amulet that kept his shifter tendencies at bay. The one notable exception had been during the summer solstice, when the magical river had crested and caused all manner of problems for anyone with a speck of magic. For those with a greater amount, the effects had been much more pronounced. PJ had nearly burnt up his pillow by the time Bev arrived with a healing crumble. But his mother had kept him home, and no one else had known.

Right?

Once they were safely in the root cellar, Bev motioned for Pip to hand over the letter. She read it five times before sighing and folding it up.

"I have to drop out," Pip said. "I was coming to tell Petula—"

"You can't drop out," Bev said then added a little sadly, "I was going to vote for you."

"Bev, this is serious. No one knew PJ was a shifter. But clearly someone does." He ran a hand over his hair nervously. "I haven't told Holly yet. She'd be on the road to Sheepsburg before I could stop her." He made a face and shook his head. "I bet it was one of his friends who blabbed to someone they shouldn't have. They're always up to no good.

Probably had too much to drink, and—"

"Pip, they'd protect PJ with their lives," Bev said. Grant Hamblin and Valta Climber had even taken great pains to distract the soldier who was about to arrest PJ before he transformed. She doubted they'd be so careless with their best friend's dangerous secret.

"Then..." He licked his lips and met her gaze nervously. "Did you tell anyone?"

Bev swallowed, once again replaying every conversation quickly. "I don't think I did."

"Can you be sure?" Pip asked.

Bev thought a little longer then nodded. "PJ is a child, and if anyone found out... I've never once pinned any of the building demolitions on PJ, and I don't even think I even mentioned there was a dragon shifter in town to anyone except..."

Lillie. She'd said her villain days were over, but was that true? Could she have, in passing, mentioned the dragon shifter in town, and Wilda put two and two together? How far would Wilda go to win?

"I have to drop out. Really no other option, is there?" Pip ran his hand over his face. "It's not worth it. Not to PJ. Not when he's about to start school. If they wanted me to quit the election, they got their wish." He shook his head. "The only reason I was running was to...well..." He chuckled. "Hendry's using her magic all the time without consequences, you know? I thought if I was mayor, it might give PJ a bit more cover. I could steer soldiers away from him, or..."

Bev bit her lip. Could *Hendry* have sent the letter? Of all the candidates, she was the most willing to do whatever it took to win, as evidenced by her behavior already. Could she have been so threatened by Pip's entry that she resorted to blackmail?

"I think you should reconsider. Maybe not be so hasty in quitting," Bev said. "Take this letter to Petula, and—"

"Are you kidding?" He jumped back in surprise, as if she were a snake that had tried to bite. "The *last* thing I want is to tell a *member of the Queen's Service* my son is a dragon!"

"Well, I'm not saying that, but you can tell her you've gotten a threat," Bev said. "Perhaps be a little vague with what it was. She's in town to monitor the election. Surely, she'd want to know that one of the candidates is being threatened."

He shook his head. "No. I'll tell you, but... I'm not risking anyone else finding out about PJ. One slipup, and Dag Flanigan is knocking at this door."

"Maybe then we focus on the candidates," Bev said. "Who has the most to gain by you dropping out?"

He shrugged. "They'd all be happy to hear it, to be honest. None of them were pleased after last night. I think Gore Dewey's gonna stop selling me horseshoes, especially after Alice stood up from Freddie's group to sign my petition." He smiled, though there wasn't much happiness in it. "Just a shame, you know? Seems folks are looking for another option." He sighed and looked out the root cellar door. "Suppose I should get up there and tell Petula before too much time passes."

Bev put her hand on his arm. "Give me a day, or at least a few hours. Let me ask around," Bev said. "Even if you do decide to drop out, we need to find out who knows PJ's secret. They might know others, too, and who knows what they'll do with that information given the chance."

"I need to work up the courage to tell Holly about this," Pip said after a moment's thought. "Once I do, she's going to tell me to drop out. But maybe…if you can figure out who it is before, and get them to forget about my son, I might be convinced to stay in."

Bev had no clue how to accomplish either of those things, but her first stop was to speak with Lillie. She'd have to be careful what she said, and how she said it, so as to not inadvertently reveal PJ's secret. It would certainly be a tricky line to walk.

Bev rapped on the door to Wilda's house and was once again met by a flurry of activity. Stella appeared much less happy to see Bev today, perhaps having heard that the inn wasn't available for a campaign event this evening, but let her in anyway.

"I need to speak with Lillie," Bev said, scanning the room. The baker was in the kitchen, unsurprisingly, icing individual cupcakes with purple and yellow frosting.

Lillie straightened at Bev's voice and frowned. "Be right there." She undid her apron and left it in the kitchen, following Bev out the door onto the front porch. "What's up? Is something wrong?"

Bev told her in hushed tones about Pip and the letter, being careful only to mention that it had been a threatening letter, that it was about someone in the family, and nothing more.

Lillie's eyes widened, and she put her hands to her mouth. "Are you *serious*? Who would..." She made a face. "Hendry."

"Yes, she's my next stop," Bev said. "But, erm..." She cleared her throat. "You didn't *tell* anyone why I was delivering crumbles at the solstice, did you? Or to whom?"

She shook her head. "I didn't mention it to anyone. Because then they might ask me why *I* needed it, you know? I was nervous enough with Zed." She chewed her lip. "What kind of magic does Pip's family have? And who?" She paused, wrinkling her nose. "On second thought, don't tell me. I don't need to know."

"Needless to say, Pip's quite beside himself," Bev

said. "He's given me a few hours, but if I don't find out who's threatening his family, he'll drop out."

Lillie tutted. "Poor Pip. He was polling so well. I bet he was going to win."

"Someone conducted a poll?" Bev said, a little surprised.

"Well, it's Shasta walking around asking questions," Lillie said with a laugh. "Wilda paid her a gold coin to ask the first twenty people she saw who they were voting for. Nearly every one was for Pip."

"So someone has a real motive to kick him out of the race," Bev said, looking out onto Wilda's garden. "It's got to be one of the other candidates."

"It's not Wilda." Lillie paused, seeming to read Bev's mind. "Or me, for that matter." She leaned in. "To be honest, I'm, er…well, I'm only helping Wilda because I live with her. Kind of hard to avoid the campaign when the headquarters is five steps from my bedroom door, you know?"

Bev nodded. "And Wilda doesn't seem like she's willing to do whatever it takes to win?"

"No. At least, not that I can tell. And unless she knows something I don't, I can't see why she'd want to send a letter like that to Pip—"

"Who sent a letter to Mr. Norris?"

Bev and Lillie jumped. Petula stood at the end of the short walkway from the road, clipboard and shiny pin in hand. She let herself into the front yard through the gate and approached them with pursed lips.

"I spoke to Mr. Norris, actually. I was letting him know his candidate petition passed muster, and he indicated he might be dropping out of the race." Petula turned her intense glare on Bev. "What's that about?"

"You'll have to ask Pip," Bev said with a thin smile.

"I did. He said he was reconsidering the amount of work involved." She adjusted her clipboard. "Which I find odd, considering the number of people who jumped up to support him last night. It seems to me someone might be pressuring him to drop out."

"Oh?" Lillie's voice was high, and Bev glared at her.

"I told all the candidates I wasn't in the mood for shenanigans this week," Petula said. "So if you know something, I suggest you tell me, so we can put a stop to it."

Bev licked her lips. "Whether Pip drops out is his decision. But I, for one, hope he doesn't."

Petula looked at Lillie, scrutinizing her with the fire of a thousand suns. Lillie's cheeks went bright pink, and she held up her hands. "I'm baking cookies for Wilda. I know nothing."

"Hm." She pulled out a sheet of paper and thrust it at Lillie. "This is Wilda's official notice that most of her signatures were valid. Unfortunately, I believe *yours* wasn't, because we couldn't find a record of you living in Pigsend for the past year."

"Oh, I haven't." Lillie's cheeks grew even darker. "Perhaps only the past four months. Right, Bev?"

Bev nodded. "Seems about right. You spent a month in the inn then moved in with Wilda around the wedding."

"Well, as per the Pigsend charter, only citizens who've lived in Pigsend the past calendar year prior to the election are eligible to sign a candidate's petition and vote in the election." Petula smiled at Lillie, but there wasn't much friendliness in it. "You are, of course, welcome to work on the campaign if you like. But unfortunately, that's where your contributions must end."

"One less vote for Wilda, I suppose," Lillie said with a sigh. "Thank you for telling me, Ms. Petula. I'm sorry I didn't know." She nodded to the paper Petula still held out in front of her. "Do you want me to deliver that to Wilda?"

"If you would. I've got to head out of town to deliver Mr. Silver's." She adjusted her tunic again. "I've already gone to Mayor Hendry. And, as I said, Mr. Norris." She paused, giving Lillie a once-over. "I want to reiterate my desire for this election to happen without any funny business, Ms...?"

"Dean," Bev said. "But I don't think she meant anything by it. None of us have read the town charter—"

"Really? I would think it would be the first thing a new citizen would read." Petula glanced between the two of them. "Well, I suppose people have different priorities. In any case, I've got to get a move on. Lots to inspect and evaluate today."

She turned and walked away, but it wasn't until she'd completely disappeared around the corner that Lillie spoke again.

"If I hear or see anything suspicious, I'll let you know," she said to Bev. "I may be on Wilda's side politically, but if someone's out there holding secrets worth threatening Pip over, it's in everyone's interest to know who it is."

~

Bev was satisfied with Lillie's answers, and confident her pobyd friend would keep a good ear out within Wilda's campaign headquarters. She doubted Wilda would come out and announce she was blackmailing her fellow candidates, but things had a way of slipping out.

As Petula was headed to Freddie's, Bev took a detour to the town hall to speak with Hendry. Once again, she was struck by the difference in atmosphere from Wilda's packed house to Hendry's quiet office, although the mayor wasn't in it. Only Sheriff Rustin, who worked across the town hall from Hendry, was there. He waved at Bev as she passed his office and smiled brightly.

"What a week for an election, eh? I'm glad I don't have to deal with any of that nonsense. Canvassing and polling and whatnot."

"Is that where Hendry is?" Bev asked, nodding to the empty office.

"I suppose. She never really tells me anything, you know." He sat back, smiling at Bev with the vapid sort of look she'd come to expect from him. "How are things at the inn? Busy?"

"A guest or two passing through a night," Bev said, looking around absentmindedly. "Say, Rustin, has Mayor Hendry mentioned any sort of... information she has on anyone?"

"Whatever do you mean?"

Bev didn't really know how to phrase it. "Just wondering if you'd heard her campaign strategy. It doesn't seem she's targeting the folks that live within Pigsend town limits. Just curious if she's...well, if she thinks she'll win."

"It's Hendry. Of course she'll win!" Rustin said with a laugh. "She does it every election. Though I suppose she's never had this many opponents. Between you and me, I think Pip Norris is going to give her a run for her money. She wasn't expecting him, I tell you that."

Bev's interest piqued. "She wasn't?"

"Not at all." He leaned in. "She's been gathering information on Wilda and Freddie for weeks, you know. Has me doing all kinds of things. But Pip?

Oh, the look on her face when he stood up and announced his candidacy was priceless. Thought she was going to burst a blood vessel." He sat back, oblivious to how incriminating the story was. "In any case, I know it's going to be a busy day for you, what with Hendry's event at the inn this evening."

Bev slapped her hand to her forehead. *Of course.* She'd actually forgotten with all the worry about Pip and his letter. "You know, I bet that's where Hendry is. Getting ready. Should head over there and help her."

He rubbed his hands together. "I hear you're making a cherry pie for her. Can't wait to taste it. Been hankering for something sweet like that for a while. I hear you made an incredible strawberry rhubarb crumble for the solstice. Shame I missed it."

Bev nodded, already inching toward the door. She did have a lot to get on with this evening, especially as she had no clue what Hendry was ordering from the butchers—or how much. "Well, if you see Hendry, let her know I need to chat with her. That is, of course, assuming she's not at the inn. Erm. Yes." Bev laughed nervously. "Headed there now."

Chapter Six

Bev hurried back to the inn. When she got there, she found the front room transformed with banners and signs proclaiming Hendry's candidacy, along with the mayor herself, who was hanging everything alone.

Bev tried to ignore the nail holes in her wall as Hendry hummed to herself happily. "Glad you're back, Bev dear. Was thinking you might be avoiding me."

"Why would you say that?" Bev asked, crossing the room to scratch Biscuit behind the ears. "I've been running errands today."

"Yes, well, it's nearly midday, and the ovens aren't even on to make your bread," Hendry said, her tone light but with an underpinning of worry. "Can't have an inn full of people without any bread to serve them."

"How many folks are you expecting, exactly?" Bev asked. "Because I've got three loaves ready to bake, but—"

"I'll need at least five," Hendry said with a wave of her hand. "If you need more gold, then—"

"Not gold. I need more time," Bev said. "You've only told me this morning you wanted to reserve the inn. Due to the temperatures, I make my bread dough the night before these days."

"Oh, that's fine. But you should get a move on. There's a pie to make, side dishes to prepare." She chuckled. "Why am I telling you? I'm sure you know all this." She turned back to the banners. "Don't mind me. I'll be working on this out here."

Bev watched her for a moment, torn, then decided to come right out with it. "Pip Norris got a threatening letter this morning. Do you know anything about that?"

She stopped and spun slowly. "Threatening? What kind of threat? Pip and Holly are about as boring as they come. Was it about their miscreant son?"

Bev swallowed her defense of PJ, opting to keep the focus on the letter. "He didn't provide specifics. But he's shaken up enough to reconsider his candidacy. I told him I'd ask around—"

"As you are our resident blackmail-solver," she said with a wink. "I hear you did great things for the Witzels."

Bev narrowed her gaze. "And how do you know about that?"

"It was *all* Ida would talk about for three weeks," Hendry said. "Bev, you don't think *I* had anything to do with this nefarious letter, do you?"

"I do, actually." Bev put her hands on her hips. "You haven't really been acting all that fair the past few days. It wouldn't be out of character—"

"I'm hurt, Bev." Hendry put a hand over her heart. "Do you really think I'd stoop so low? I told you the other day, I plan to win fair and square." She adjusted her tunic. "But if I *were* going to pin the blame on someone, Wilda Murtagh would probably do something that underhanded. You *do* remember who she's related to, don't you?"

"The mayor of Middleburg," Bev said, a little tiredly.

"And you remember all the chaos they got up to during the Harvest Festival last year, don't you?"

"I remember a lot of it was caused by a certain soldier masquerading as a judge," Bev said. "And I still lost to what's-his-name from Middleburg."

"Yes, because he can't read a room and stayed around instead of slinking back to that dastardly city with the rest of them after they tried to *ruin* our festival so Petula would move it to their town,"

Hendry said. "In any case, your focus should probably be on Wilda. I'm sure she'd like to snap up some of those folks who stood and threw their lot in with Pip." She turned back to the banners. "After, of course, you make the dinner for my campaign event tonight. I've already paid the butchers, but I'm sure Ida could use some help bringing it all over."

"So you're not worried about Ida poisoning your meat?" Bev said with a little chuckle.

"Oh, beggars can't be choosers. Not as if there are a plethora of butchers around town. Besides, I'm sure you'll cook out any poison that goes into it, hm?" Hendry turned back to her banners. "I'd head over there soon, though. The day is wearing on, you know!"

Bev didn't like being ordered around, but Hendry did have a point, so she crossed the street to check in with Ida. Unsurprisingly, Vellora was working on Freddie's campaign for the day, a fact that both vexed and amused Ida.

"I honestly don't care who wins," Ida said, "but Vellora's intent on Freddie. Thinks he's going to bring *real change* to Pigsend." She mimicked Vellora's lower voice. "I said, change for what? What does Hendry even *do* all day, other than ruin your life by making you do her job, Bev?"

Bev shrugged, keeping quiet in case Ida dropped information that could lead to Pip's blackmailer.

"And I told her, 'Gore's his campaign manager.

Why are you always over there?' And *she* tells me that it's comeuppance for all the time I spend on the Harvest Festival—you know I'm hoping to chair it again this year—and while that's all well and good, the Harvest Festival is at least going to result in something. If Freddie Silver wins the mayoral election, I'll dunk my head in Pigsend Creek."

Bev quirked a brow. "You don't think he'll win?"

"I think he's got an uphill battle, especially now that Pip's in the race," Ida said. "Nobody's going to vote for Wilda Murtagh. So in my mind, it's really a race between Freddie and Pip."

It was becoming quite clear that whichever camp Bev was talking to was convinced *they* were the one tied with Pip.

"I'm sure you two will navigate it well," Bev said, after a long pause. "Does Freddie seem… Well, I don't really know him, I suppose. Never really needed to chat with him about anything. What do you know about him?"

"I'm not exactly sure how he got so close with Vellora," Ida said with a shrug. "You know the Silvers grow mostly wheat on their farm, so we don't really visit all that often. I have a hunch Freddie might've been in the war at one point, so maybe they reminisce about that."

Bev nodded. That was certainly true. She didn't like that she knew more about Vellora's rebellious activities in the dark forest than Ida did, but Vellora had her reasons for keeping secrets from Ida.

Ida continued rambling on about Freddie, the campaign, and what she thought, as Bev considered Freddie Silver as a potential culprit. His husband had needed a bite of rhubarb crumble, which presumably meant he had some magic. Would Freddie stoop so low as to threaten another magical family in town? It was…unlikely. But Bev had learned nothing was ever as it seemed when it came to people.

"Well, suppose I've got to let you get back to it," Ida said. "You've got a lot of meat to cook." She thumbed to the back room. "Goodness. I do hope there's a crowd tonight. Otherwise, all this work for nothing, eh?"

~

By the time Bev and Ida had brought all the meat over, Hendry had finished her preparations— even gone to the farmers' market to get cherries, potatoes, and carrots—and had left for the rest of the afternoon. That suited Bev fine, as she had a lot of work to do. She dressed and seasoned the lamb, getting it in the oven to cook, then turned to her Victory Cherry Pie, as Hendry had termed it. Bev didn't make sweets, generally, but Wim did have a few recipe cards for pies and crumbles that were good in a pinch.

She started with the crusts, combining flour, cold butter from the root cellar, and a little water until she managed a nice crust—enough for three pies. She rolled that into a ball and stashed it back in the root cellar, next turning to the cherries. They were a beautiful color, still plump from all the excess magic a few weeks ago, and would probably taste incredible no matter what she did to them. First, though, she needed to get the pits out. Lillie had given her a piping tip to tackle the job, and that worked quite well. Within half an hour, she'd pitted all the cherries and gotten them into the mixture with sugar and a little lemon to marinate while she retrieved the crust.

She rolled it out on the table, but before she could get the first one into its tin, Petula knocked on the kitchen door.

"May I have a word with you, Bev?" she asked.

"Sure." Bev rolled the dough onto her pin and laid it on top of the pie plate. "What's up?"

"I'm concerned about Mr. Norris," Petula said, watching Bev cut off the excess pie crust. "Now, I know I'm an outsider, and sometimes that can cause people to be suspicious. But my job is to ensure the election occurs fairly, and I can't do that until I know what's going on."

Bev sighed, reaching for the filling and pouring it into the unbaked crust. "He got a letter that spooked him. Someone wanting him to drop out. I don't know specifics."

"I suspected as much. Not the first time such a

thing has happened, you know." Petula sniffed, and it almost sounded like a chuckle. "There've been several elections I've been a part of where letters and threatening comments have surfaced. Which is why Her Majesty's put so much effort into ensuring that local elections are monitored. Rural towns like this can sometimes feel so remote from Queen's Capital that the local politicians might believe they can pull the wool over their constituents' eyes. But we're not going to let that happen, are we, Bev?"

"Wait. We?" Bev blinked.

"Yes." She cleared her throat. "As I said, it's clear the locals don't quite trust me to investigate, as they don't want to give me details. But they've got trust in you. It's grown even since I was last here." She laughed. "I daresay if you were running for mayor, you'd have even Mr. Norris beat."

Bev didn't even want to consider that scenario. "What about Rustin? He's the sheriff."

"Well, as, erm, *qualified* as he is, I'm afraid he's pretty clearly been added to Hendry's team," she said. "Not to mention, you're already looking into the situation, aren't you? Isn't that what I overheard you speaking about with Ms. Dean?"

Bev nodded. "It's obviously one of the other candidates, or someone who works for them. But I can't figure out who knows..." She stopped herself in time. "Who would have information on Pip. He's so...dull." She was using Hendry's words, but they fit the picture of the farrier. "And well-liked."

"Everyone seems to have their secrets. Perhaps if you can figure out *what* secret Mr. Norris is hiding, that will lead you to the culprit." She beamed. "I have all the faith in the world that you'll complete this task, Bev."

~

Petula might've had faith in Bev, but she was starting to doubt herself. The hours ticked on, and everything got into the oven, but other than speaking with Lillie and getting the runaround from Hendry, Bev hadn't really learned anything about Pip's blackmailer. It was hard to suss out a secret without divulging the secret, and for once, Bev found herself staring at the ticking clock without a clue what to do.

When it struck six, Bev brought out the veritable feast, only to find the crowd somewhat thinner than anticipated. Only three faces, to be exact, smiled back at her, though Hendry's was more of a grimace. The others, Bardoff and Rustin, looked unperturbed that the crowd was so small and eager to hear from their illustrious leader.

"Just put it down," Hendry said. "We'll have our fill."

"I'm sure Earl and Etheldra will be along in a minute," Bev said, glancing at the time. "Suppose they're delayed a little."

"No, they aren't coming. Earl told me," Bardoff

said. "Can't imagine why."

Hendry gestured to the spread. "Come now, help yourselves, gentlemen. Bev certainly went to a lot of trouble to make all this food. Can't let it go to waste."

Bev couldn't help but feel for the mayor as her only two supporters plated their dinners and returned to the single table. She'd had small crowds before, but it felt even smaller with all the banners and decorations that had been hung for no one. She also was no stranger to making a feast for a crowd that didn't show, although that happened less frequently, but something about Hendry hovering over the food table, still overflowing, broke Bev's heart a little.

At fifteen past, the front door opened, and Hendry's face lit up with excitement, only to fall as Petula rushed in, adjusting her pin and smiling.

"So sorry I'm late," she said. "Got caught up down at Wilda's. She's having a raucous good time, and—" She stopped, glancing around at the sparsely attended event. "Well, erm. I'm here now. Please, don't let me interrupt things."

"Nothing to interrupt," Hendry said darkly, turning away from Petula as she surveyed the food once more, as if it were the cause of the lack of participation. "Please, have something to eat."

"I'm quite stuffed. The bakers had a scrumptious quiche, and..." Petula once again cleared her throat.

"In any case, please feel free to begin your event whenever you like."

Hendry sighed. "Who else is having an event?"

"I believe Mr. Silver is having his at his farm. I've got to stop by there in a bit. And Mr. Norris is having one at his neighbor Earl's house."

That certainly explained their absence.

"His workshop would be a nice space. It's quite open these days," Bev said.

"All well attended?" Hendry asked, running a finger along the line of her lip color.

"Erm, yes. Unfortunately. Seems the town is split evenly between them." Petula made a sound as she rose. "Are you going to be giving a speech this evening?"

Hendry's smile was tight. "No one to give a speech to."

"I'd love to hear a speech," Bardoff said with a bright smile—one that quickly dimmed as Hendry scowled at him.

"Well, if that's the case," Petula said gently. "I might head over to Mr. Norris's event. He promised he would wait until I got there to give his speech."

"Is he...feeling better about his campaign?" Bev asked. "If he's having a rally, I'd wager he is."

"Suppose so." Petula crossed the room to where Hendry stood, and the election monitor patted her on the shoulder. "You know, dear, sometimes a change of pace is good for us, hm? I thought my career was over when I was demoted to Harvest Festival events. But with hard work, and a strict adherence to the rules, I managed to get right back into election monitoring."

Hendry's eyes grew cold. "Is that supposed to make me feel better?"

Petula dropped her hand and turned to the rest. "Well, Ms. Bev, I'll see you later on this evening, I suppose. Don't wait up for me. Goodness knows I'll be crisscrossing all three events this evening until the wee hours."

She left quickly, resulting in a dull silence that Bev found somewhat unbearable. "Shall I—"

"Rustin," Hendry said, after a moment, "who's catering Pip's party? Anyone know?"

"I don't think anyone," Rustin said with a frown. "The inn's all booked up. The butchers are down at Freddie's, and the bakers are at Wilda's. Don't know of anyone who'd be on Pip's side who'd want to cook for them."

"What are you thinking?" Bev asked.

"It would be a shame for all this food to go to waste. Especially that beautiful cherry pie," Hendry said with a smile. "Come. Let's bring it to Pip's."

Chapter Seven

Rustin and Bardoff didn't mind being impressed into service, with Rustin carrying the platter of meat as well as a large stack of Bev's wooden plates, and Bardoff juggling both bowls of vegetables, the basket of bread, and the utensils. Bev carried the pies, and Hendry, predictably, carried nothing except her own plans as she marched them through town toward Earl's. It wasn't a very long walk, but Bev spent all of it wondering what the mayor was up to.

The torchlights shone and conversations echoed long before the group arrived at Earl's house. His entire back yard, including his workshop, was filled with people milling around. There was a makeshift stage and podium, presumably made by the carpenter himself, and a banner proclaiming Pip's candidacy. But said candidate wasn't anywhere to be found. Bev spotted Jane Medlam, the mason, Trent Scrawl, a farmer, and others, but no Pip or Holly.

"Where's Pip?" Bev asked.

But the answer to that had to wait, as Hendry was met at the entrance by Earl, who wore a look of consternation that was very unlike him.

"What are you doing here?" Earl snapped. "Come to ruin our party? Shut us down for some unknown noise violation?"

"My dear Earl," Hendry said with a laugh as she gestured to the group behind her. "I'm here to spread the love. Bev made this meal for my event, but I'm sorry to say, my attendees weren't very hungry. Goodness knows Freddie Silver's home is too far of a walk, and I wouldn't be caught dead bringing anything but a plague to Wilda's house." She cracked a smile. "And I thought, with such short notice, Pip might be in need of some extra food."

Earl listened to all this with a suspicious glare, and Bev couldn't blame him.

"Is this all who came to your event, then?" Earl asked, nodding to the group behind her.

Hendry waved her hand. "Many others, of course, but they had to get back to their farms. The folks out in the rural parts of town forgot that our beloved inn is renowned for its food, and they'd already eaten."

Bev clicked her tongue, amazed how well Hendry could tell a baldfaced lie. But that probably came with the territory of being a politician.

"In any case, this food is going to go to waste, and my dear Rustin's arms are about to fall off from carrying it across town," Hendry said. "So where shall I put it?"

Earl met Bev's gaze, and she nodded approvingly. "It's all freshly cooked, Earl. Promise."

"Fine. Go put it over there." He gestured to a table where a few baskets of fruit had been set. It certainly *wasn't* the spread Hendry had ordered, but with the addition of the chicken, side dishes, and cherry pies, it was much more inviting.

"I'm *so* glad this worked out," Hendry announced as Rustin, Bardoff, and Bev set everything down. "Tell me this is only what's left, not what was served?"

Earl's cheeks went pink. "This is fine."

"This isn't *fine*, Earl." Hendry laughed as people came closer, drawn by the scent of fresh-cooked chicken, bread, and the delicious pies. "Please, come eat. You all look positively *starved*. Come, come." She placed a soft hand on the first in the queue.

Jane didn't recoil at her touch. "What's all this?"

"Food from the Weary Dragon," Hendry said, making sure her voice carried across the crowd. "Yes, Etheldra, I've brought your dinner to you. We did miss you tonight."

Etheldra scowled but didn't come closer.

"Oh, Willhem, it's so lovely to see you. Traveled in from the north, did you?" She beamed at the farmer, who seemed surprised Hendry knew them. "I see little Tallulah at school all the time. She's growing like a weed, isn't she?"

Willhem nodded, a little uncertainly.

Hendry moved them forward then held out her hand to Grant Klose, peppering him with questions about his harvest, then to Mandisa Munson, asking if she was planning on submitting her jams to the Harvest Festival again. On and on, until it was plainly apparent that Hendry knew every single thing about every person in the crowd. Was it her politician's knowledge, or was she using her magic to scrape the minds of everyone she touched? Bev certainly hadn't felt the mayor use any magic this evening, but just because Hendry hadn't used it on Bev didn't mean she wasn't using it on the rest of the town.

Hendry worked the crowd as if this were *her* campaign event, and as the plates filled with food and smiles loosened, Earl's scowl grew more pronounced.

"Didn't think I'd need to *feed* everyone," he grumbled to Bev. "This is real nice, Bev. Crashing our party like this. A little surprised you'd agree to helping Hendry."

"I promise, I had no clue what she was up to," Bev said, holding up her hands. "And in any case, she's right. All this food would've gone to waste had we not brought it."

"How many people were actually at her event?" Earl asked.

Bev glanced at Hendry, who was still glad-handing and ignoring them. Then she pointed at Rustin and Bardoff, the latter two who were also serving themselves happily.

Earl snorted and shook his head, folding his arms over his chest. "Suppose that's for the best, then. Nobody here's going to vote for her, no matter how well she feeds them. But at least people will hang around until Pip gives his speech."

Bev tried to look neutral. "So he's still planning on doing that?"

"Why wouldn't he?" Earl frowned.

If Pip hadn't told his own wife about the threatening letters, she doubted he'd told his campaign manager. "It's getting late, you know? Would've thought he'd be out here mingling."

"Oh, Earl!" Hendry called, walking over. "You certainly did draw a crowd, didn't you? Whatever were you going to do if we hadn't shown up with all this food? We might not even have enough for everyone. My victory cherry pies are all but gone— thanks to Rustin, that scoundrel." She laughed, and it echoed through the space, earning a growl from

Earl. "In any case, we *do* seem to be running low on plates. Do you know where we can rustle some up?"

"I'll get more from Pip's," Earl said.

"Where is our beloved farrier?" Hendry asked, her eyes wide with mirth. "Don't tell me he's late to his own party."

"He's working on his speech," Earl shot back. "Anyway. Thanks for the food. Don't think it's necessary for you to stick around, Hendry."

"I absolutely think it's necessary," Hendry said with a laugh. "Let's see what Pip has to say. Best to know one's competition, you know?"

"I'll head over to Pip's," Bev said. "See what he's got available for plates and a serving spoon." She smiled convincingly at Earl. "You can stay here and…manage the food queue."

Keep an eye on Hendry was the unsaid part of that, and Earl nodded appreciatively. Bev turned on her heel, walked through the crowd of at least thirty-five people, and hopped the fence between Earl's and Pip's yards to jog up the front steps. She rapped on their front door, waiting for a moment. When no one answered, she rapped again.

"Pip? Holly? It's Bev," she said. "Just here to—"

The door swung open, and Holly's face was ashen gray. She said nothing and all but yanked Bev into the house.

"What—" Bev stopped, spotting Pip with a letter in hand. "Don't tell me you got another one."

He nodded. "This one was handed to Holly sometime at the party tonight. She didn't see who. Too many people."

Bev chewed her lip. "What does it say?"

"It says...*I'm going to tell your campaign manager what really happened to his barn*." Holly was on the verge of tears. "How long have *you* known about these letters, Bev?"

"Since this morning," Bev said. "I told Pip I'd look into it."

"And?"

Bev shook her head. "I don't have any suspects. Well, I *do* have suspects, but no leads. Your candidates have motivation, as evidenced by the party outside."

"What's Hendry doing here?" Holly snapped, looking out the window.

"Her campaign event was...sparsely attended," Bev said, deciding she didn't owe it to Hendry to lie. "So she decided to bring the food I made here instead."

"Why?" Pip frowned. "I'm her competition."

"To be honest, I'm not sure," Bev said. "She certainly told Earl she had more than Rustin and Bardoff, so I'm not sure if she's trying to save face, or maybe..." Bev nodded to the letter. "Maybe she knows what's coming."

"It would be her, wouldn't it?" Holly said with a nasty glare out the window. "She'd do anything to save her own skin."

"I don't actually know if it's her," Bev said. "Because I don't know who knows about PJ's secret. It should be no one."

"Should be," Holly said. "But it clearly isn't. I spoke with my sister, and she swears it wasn't her, either. But who knows?" She shook her head. "Word gets around."

Apolinary wouldn't put her nephew in danger like that, nor would Grant and Valta. Bev desperately wished she had an answer for them, but all she could do was watch in silence.

"Suppose that's it, then," Pip said with a sigh. "Earl's gonna kill me. And I can't tell him why, either. We're on such good terms. He'd never forgive me for what Pip did to his workshop."

"Better Earl upset than our son in the queen's clutches," Holly said firmly.

~

Bev followed Pip and Holly outside, their grim faces in stark contrast to the raucous applause that met them. Bev's gaze went to Hendry, who was a little too smug. Bev's suspicions were raised once again. Had she sent the letters then come to the scene of the crime to sweep up voters once Pip was out of the race?

She was still glad-handing and making sure everyone knew *she* was the one to sweep in and save Pip's first campaign event. Bev overheard her lamenting that a campaign event was a good precursor to how a candidate would run their administration and that it was *so* important for a candidate to know what they were doing.

"You can't tell me she's not responsible for this," Holly whispered harshly to Bev.

"I told you. I'm looking into it," Bev said. "Are you sure I can't get you to reconsider, Pip?"

"No. Holly's right." He looked down at the speech he'd handwritten on a scrap of paper. "PJ's safety is more important."

He climbed onto the stage, coming to the podium and looking like he was going to be sick. Holly stood beside him, her lips pressed into a thin line. Earl's brow was furrowed in worry, but Pip waved him away, taking a deep breath before facing the crowd with a smile.

"Wait, wait!" Petula's voice rang out from somewhere in the crowd. "So sorry I'm late." She pushed her way through, coming to stand at the front. "Please tell me you haven't started your speech yet, Pip?"

"No, just about to," he said.

"Excellent." She adjusted the pin on her shirt. "Please, don't let me keep you from it."

Pip smoothed the paper on the podium. "First and foremost, I wanted to say thank you for all the support—"

A loud cheer rose from the crowd, and he

looked even more ill.

"Suppose I should get this out of the way," he muttered. "Anyway, thanks for the support, but I'm dropping out of the race."

A loud cheer rose up from the crowd again, as they perhaps hadn't heard him. But Earl had, jumping up from his spot and rushing the stage to speak with Pip in hushed tones. Pip spoke back, shaking his head wildly.

"What's going on?" Etheldra came to stand next to Bev. She had a small piece of cherry pie in her hand. "Excellent pie, by the way. The bread leaves a little to be desired. Sliced too thinly, if you ask me."

"Pip's dropping out," Bev said, nodding to the stage.

"Why?" Etheldra narrowed her gaze.

"I'm sure he'll tell us in a moment," Bev said.

"What do *you* know, Bev?" The tea shop owner's gaze was intense. "Because you always *know* these things before they come out."

Bev turned, her interest piqued at the emphasis on the word *know*. Did Etheldra know about PJ? She always had insight into the secrets Bev wanted to keep quiet about, like Lillie being a pobyd.

"Hm?" Etheldra prompted. "Well?"

"I'd ask what you know, Etheldra?" Bev countered. "Keen for Pip to drop out so Earl will stop being his campaign manager?"

"Are you joking? It's given him something to do

that's *not* coming up with ridiculous projects at my house and shop." She finished the cherry pie and swallowed. "You should know better than to suspect me, Bev."

"What am I suspecting you of?" Bev asked.

"Well, I *assume* since Pip's dropping out of the race, someone has some kind of dirt on him that's convinced him to call it quits." She tilted her head. "Or did I mishear you?"

Pip finally managed to get away from Earl and addressed the crowd again, who had, by now, talked amongst themselves and figured out what he'd said.

"Anyway, I'm so grateful for all your support," he said. "But I was too hasty, putting my hat in the ring, you know? I'm not a mayor or a politician. Just a simple farrier. And erm…anyway."

"I think," Hendry's voice rang out clearly through the crowd, "that it might be beneficial for you to throw your support in with another candidate." She smiled proudly. "If you aren't going to be in it yourself, your supporters want to know who's got *your* backing."

"I'm not ready to make that decision," Pip said darkly. "And in any case, I think there's a reason two other folks signed up to run. Clearly, the people of Pigsend don't think you've done a good job."

Hendry's face fell. Not the ringing endorsement she'd obviously been hoping for.

"In any case, I'm sorry for getting your hopes

up," Pip said. "And when I know who's going to get my vote in three days, I'll let you know. But in the meantime…erm…the party's over. You guys should go home."

Chapter Eight

Pip and Holly disappeared into their house, and some of the crowd dispersed, but most everyone stayed, holding their plates and talking amongst themselves about what had transpired. Everyone in the crowd looked stunned, upset, concerned—everyone except Hendry.

She'd shaken off Pip's words and was working the crowd once more, offering her opinion about amateur politicians, but it fell on deaf ears. After a few tries and fails, she switched tactics, commiserating with them about their disappointment then asking who they thought they might vote for. Unsurprisingly, no one in attendance said her.

"Well," Hendry adjusted her tunic, "suppose I should go talk with Pip. Make sure he's all right."

"I wouldn't," Bev said, glaring at her. "I think you've done enough tonight, haven't you?"

"I brought food, Bev. Food *I* paid for." She clicked her tongue at the empty table. "If I were really rude, I'd march into Pip's and ask him to pay me back, but I'm a nice person, you know. Not one to kick someone when they're down."

But are you the one who knocked them down in the first place?

"In any case, it doesn't appear you'll get any voters here tonight, so you probably should move on. Head home."

"If you *insist*." Hendry snapped her fingers at Bardoff and Rustin, who were having a lovely conversation with Alice. "You two. Come. We've got work to do."

Bev realized too late that the mayor wasn't going to help her carry all the dirty dishes back to the inn, and she scowled at the mayor's retreating back.

"Suppose I'd better start getting this back, then," Bev said with a sigh as she piled the dirty dishes onto the empty platter.

"I'll help," Alice said.

Herman Monday, standing next to her, nodded. "Me, too."

The journey back to the inn was much less precarious than the one there, but there was plenty of conversation about Pip's abrupt mind change.

"I mean, you heard him. He realized what he was getting into and decided he didn't want to do it," Herman said, holding the empty platter of chicken grease.

"I bet Hendry got to him," Alice said. "She *happened* to show up with all this food, eh? Seemed like she was primed and ready to take all the voters she could."

"What'dya reckon, Bev?" Herman asked.

Bev shook her head. "I don't know. But I know he's broken more than a few hearts with his announcement."

They continued speculating, leaving Bev alone with her thoughts. If Hendry was trying to avoid suspicion, or at least look more innocent, she was doing a poor job of it. Which almost made Bev feel she *couldn't* be behind it. Hendry was many things —cutthroat, manipulative, selfish, and far too demanding of Bev's time—but she wasn't stupid. She was keenly aware of how she appeared to others, and did whatever she could to make sure she only showed her best face.

The trio put all the dishes in Bev's sink, and she thanked them profusely for their assistance. "Not to worry, Bev, we're always happy to help," Alice said.

"Anything for you," Herman said.

Bev cleared her throat. "Are you lot headed back home, or…?"

"I hear Freddie Silver's having a big blowout tonight, too. Probably still going on," Alice said. "Not that I'm ready to pick another candidate, but if Pip's really out—"

"He looked it to me," Herman said.

"Then Freddie's my second choice," Alice said. "Not gonna vote for Wilda. Not in this lifetime, anyway."

"She isn't so bad," Herman said. "Honestly, I may head up to her house. See what she's got going on. At least she has the bakers on her side, so that probably means they'll have cookies."

"I definitely saw Lillie and Allen making some earlier," Bev said. "But I also know the Witzels are down at the Silvers', and I hear they've got a pig on a spit. So I don't think you could really go wrong with either."

Herman patted his stomach, seeming to decide. How quaint would it be if the election were decided purely on Pigsend's stomachs?

"Nah, I can buy a scone from the bakers tomorrow," Alice said. "I'm going to Freddie's."

"Suit yourself." Herman waved them off. "What about you, Bev? Gonna go get a cookie or some pork?"

Bev really should've tackled the dishes in her sink, but she owed it to Pip to start sniffing around. Lillie would keep a good eye on Wilda's party, so Freddie's would have to be it.

"I'm feeling savory," Bev said after a moment. "Shall we?"

The Silvers' farm was an even longer journey in the dark, but with Alice, at least there was good company. She, luckily, took up the lion's share of the conversation, and Bev could once again spin theories and replay every conversation she'd had since the early spring. She was *sure* no one knew about PJ, and even more sure that no one had connected the spate of building fires and demolishment with him.

No one except PJ's family and friends, of course. As confident as she was that Grant and Valta would be careful with their words, she couldn't be completely sure. Not until she asked them herself. Grant was in Sheepsburg, but Valta was still in town, if Gore was to be believed.

As with Pip's party, the raucous noise could be heard long before Bev and Alice set foot on Freddie's property. Here, the noise was aided by a trio of performers: farmer Dane Sterling, Eldred Nest, and the miller Sonny Gray, who were playing on a raised stage as loudly and joyously as their instruments would allow. There were banners proclaiming Freddie was the new, best option for Pigsend. And in front of the stage, a crowd of people were dancing and laughing as they enjoyed the music.

The scent of perfectly cooked pork wafted over,

and Bev spotted the Witzels standing next to a pig on a spit. Bev recognized the combination of spices as the Witzel family recipe, the same one they'd made for Earl and Etheldra's wedding a few weeks ago.

Ida caught her eye and waved, walking over and giving Bev a hug. "What are you doing all the way out here?"

"Just thought I'd do the rounds," Bev said.

"I take it Hendry's event was a bust?" Ida said with a knowing smirk. "I daresay half the town is here. And the other half came from Pip's event." She shook her head. "Shame that he dropped out, isn't it?"

"Mm." Bev tilted her head to Ida. "What have you heard about that?"

She frowned. "Just that it happened. Gore was all over it as soon as the first person showed up. He's in rare form, you know. Who would've thought a blacksmith would've been such a vocal campaign manager?" She chuckled. "But really, what are you doing here? Are you going to vote for Freddie?"

"Still on the fence." Bev scanned the crowd, seeing more than a few people who'd come from Pip's event. They were eating more, perhaps comparing the two meals, though there wasn't any kind of dessert. At least not that Bev could see. One mark in Wilda's favor, she supposed.

"Is Petula here?" Bev asked.

"Yeah." Ida pointed over to the corner, where the election monitor stood aloofly, watching the crowd for signs of trouble with a disapproving smile. Perhaps not a fan of music. "Suppose she was pretty surprised about Pip, too, hm?" Ida nudged Bev. "So what's really going on?"

"Why would you think I'd know?"

Ida gave her a look.

"I don't know," Bev said with a huff, "but I know that someone on one of these campaigns seems to want to play dirty. I need to figure out who it is."

"Nobody here," Ida said. "It's probably Hendry. Or Wilda. They seem cut from the same cloth."

Bev made a noise, not willing to agree or disagree with her right now. The key to sussing out the culprit would be keeping information close to the vest.

The music stopped, and Gore came to the stage, holding a set of cards in his hands. He cleared his throat and rapped his knuckles on the pole holding one of the banners, quieting the crowd. The sea of people, perhaps fifty in total, moved closer to the stage, watching him curiously.

"Welcome, everybody!" he bellowed, his deep voice echoing "I'm so glad to see everyone here this evening, especially those who're attending their *second* rally this evening." He chuckled then spotted Bev in the audience. "And Bev, I hear this is your third!"

Bev scowled as the crowd's attention swept to her but said nothing.

"I kid, I kid. I'm even happy to see you, too, Bev, even if you did waste your talents cooking for Mayor Hendry."

A chorus of boos rose from the group, and Bev was actually happy the mayor hadn't decided to crash another party. Probably not even Hendry's thick skin could take a second round of dissent.

"Yes, we've all had about enough of our current mayor's antics, haven't we?" Gore drawled, earning applause and cheers. "I think it's time Pigsend has a mayor who really cares about its people, not uses them for their own benefit."

The crowd cheered again, and even Ida clapped, nudging Bev with a meaningful look.

"I know many of you had your hearts set on Pip," Gore said. "And I can appreciate that you're looking for another answer. But if the race is between Freddie Silver, a son of Pigsend, a farmer, and a real champion for the little guy, or Wilda Murtagh—"

More boos, though not quite as many as for Hendry.

"Then I think we all know who the right choice is, eh?" He put his speech into his back pocket and clapped his hands. "Now, I know you haven't come to hear me chatter on. How's about we hear from our candidate, eh?"

This time, the cheers were the loudest they'd been, and Gore turned to the edge of the stage, where Freddie was waiting, holding his husband's hand. Hans looked nervous, much like Holly had when Pip gave his resignation, but Freddie glowed with confidence, waving to the crowd with aplomb and shaking Gore's hand firmly.

He took Gore's spot and smiled, taking a deep breath. "Good evening, Pigsend!" More cheers. "I'm so happy to be here with you this evening. Many of you have traveled a great distance to hear me speak, and I want you to know how grateful I am for that." He nodded to Petula. "And to you, Ms. Banks, for ensuring we have a fair and clean election."

Petula smiled thinly.

"As I look out across this crowd, I see a group of people hungry for change. For someone who won't let things happen to Pigsend, but who'll actually go out and solve the problems! Someone who'll roll up their sleeves and do the hard work."

He continued, and Bev lost interest in what he had to say in favor of Hans, who was talking with Gore about something off to the side. He held a piece of paper in his hand, and Bev's breath caught.

Not another one.

~

Freddie went on for at least twenty minutes, outlining some of his proposals. Bev had no clue how many of his promises were possible and how many were wishful thinking. She hadn't realized how much the farmers' daily lives were impacted by the queen's regulations, and based on Petula's expression, many of the changes Freddie was proposing wouldn't actually come to pass. But the crowd liked it, and that was something.

She kept her gaze on Hans and Gore, with Gore looking like he was trying to assuage Hans, and Hans shaking his head furiously. Finally, Freddie's speech ended to more applause, and the candidate stepped off the stage to shake hands and work the crowd. Gore left Hans alone, and Bev sensed her opportunity.

She wove through the crowd, giving brief hellos to those who recognized her, before she was able to call out to Hans. He was on his way back to their small house in the distance, his shoulders tense and his face a mask of concern.

"Hans!" Bev called.

He stopped and turned around with the barest attempt at a smile. "Bev, hi. I was headed back home. Got a bit of a headache. Think the ale we brewed might've gotten to my head."

"Did you get a letter?" Bev asked.

His eyes widened, and he took a step back. "What do you know about that?"

"You're not the only one," Bev said. "May I see it?"

He seemed like he'd rather not, but after a moment, he pulled the paper from his back pocket and handed it over. Bev scanned it quickly, finding the exact same handwriting as before.

Tell your husband to drop out of the race, or we'll tell everyone about your magic.

"I don't know what they're talking about," Hans said quickly. "Magic. I don't have magic."

"I know you do," Bev said, looking up at him. "Your husband brought you some of my crumble, remember?"

His cheeks went pink. "I s-suppose he did."

"Are you still having trouble with it?" Bev asked.

"No. Once the solstice passed, everything went back to normal." He wrung his hands. "But Bev, no one knows about my magic."

"Gore does, and the Witzels," Bev said, thinking of the people who were at the dark forest during the solstice. "And Andres, Vellora's commander."

"All people who'd be on my husband's side," he said. "In any case, Gore... Well, he thinks it's nothing. Told me not to tell my husband, as it'll only make him worry. That it's more important that Freddie win this race than..." He sighed. "And he also said it didn't matter because I don't have magic anymore."

"Is that true?" Bev asked, thinking of Allen.

"Who knows what these soldiers would come up with?" Hans said. "They tested me once upon a time, but lately, it seems they're eager to snatch up anyone with a hint of magic." He paused. "Wait, did Pip get one of these letters, too?"

Bev nodded. "Scared him enough to drop out."

"So I've got one, and Pip got one." He snorted. "I bet you a gold coin Hendry *didn't* get one."

Bev wasn't so sure about that, as the mayor also had magic to hide from the soldiers.

Hans looked at the letter again, anger replacing the concern in his gaze. "Well, in that case, I'm not going to tell my husband. If whoever it is thinks they can bully us into dropping out, they've got another think coming. I don't know what Pip's got that scared him enough to end his campaign, but Gore's right. Freddie's candidacy is important to Pigsend. And if he drops out, it's between Wilda and Hendry. That's not a choice anyone wants, is it?"

Bev nodded, looking back at the party. The question now was, who in Pigsend knew about PJ *and* Hans?

Chapter Nine

By the time Bev returned to the village, it was quite late, and although she had a mountain of dishes and a front room full of banners to remove, she went to bed. Her sleep was broken, running through everyone on Hendry and Wilda's campaign, including the candidates, as she pondered who was sending these letters.

Hendry, of course, was running her campaign herself, but she had two people aligned with her. Unless Rustin was hiding a rather *large* secret about his intelligence, she doubted it was him. Bardoff was more loyal to the status quo than Hendry herself, and while that could be a motive to send letters, he'd been gone during the solstice madness. So unless someone told him something, he wouldn't have known about Freddie.

Wilda had several folks who might be on the list—the Brewer twins had their own brush with magic, Lillie was a pobyd, Allen with his touch of pobyd magic that hadn't seemed to fade yet. Bev hadn't told any of them who else she was bringing crumbles to, or why, as that information in the wrong hands could've been catastrophic.

Then there was the wild card—someone who'd randomly seen PJ puffing smoke either during the solstice or when he'd been in the throes of his transformation *and* had coincidentally also seen Hans's magic zipping around their farmhouse. But the Silvers lived so far out of town that an accidental glimpse was quite unlikely.

Bev tried to find a connection between the two families, but it was difficult. The Silvers had horses, so Pip might've brought his son out to change their shoes, but other than that, there wasn't a time when Hans and PJ had been in the same place. Much more likely there was a piece to the puzzle missing.

The next morning, with Biscuit at her heels, she walked downstairs, grateful no one had come to stay the night before, because she wasn't in the mood to do laundry. But when she reached the landing and was confronted with Hendry's banners, she let out a frustrated sigh.

"Suppose it would be too much to ask for her to

come take these down, eh?" Bev said to Biscuit.

He let out a low sniff.

"Fine, fine. Breakfast first."

She fed her laelaps and Sin then set to clearing the decor before finishing the dishes, muttering to herself and thinking through her suspects and questions.

"Do you think Hendry did it?" Bev asked Biscuit as she unpinned one brightly-colored banner. "It really doesn't seem her style to be so sloppy."

Biscuit sniffed from his spot on the ground.

"But who knows? Maybe she did it intentionally to throw me off her scent," Bev said. "Be too sloppy about it so I wouldn't suspect her, because I know her."

He ruffed.

"You're right. I'm not making any sense, am I?" She yawned. "Maybe I need a cup of tea."

Bev set to that, and after sitting and drinking a cup of Etheldra's morning blend, her mind was a little clearer. She glanced at the clock, hoping Lillie would be the one to bring the morning's pastries— and have something of value to share about Wilda's event.

Lillie did, indeed, bring the pastries and also looked like she hadn't gotten a lick of sleep the night before. She yawned loudly as she put the muffins on the table and waved off Bev's concern.

"Wilda's party went late," she said. "I went to bed at nine, but goodness, the noise! I couldn't close my eyes until well after one. Then, of course, we were up at four to bake." She shook her head. "Honestly thought I might come get a room at the inn to sleep."

"You're certainly welcome to do that," Bev said. "Did you see anything strange last night?"

"Not particularly." Lillie thought for a moment. "Except I heard Pip dropped out. Twenty people showed up halfway through Wilda's party, spinning wild stories about Pip and Hendry." She shook her head. "Goodness, that's right. Hendry had her rally here last night. How did it go?"

Bev told her about Hendry's lackluster event and her not-so-brilliant idea to bring her uneaten food to Pip's. "Pip got another letter, this one given to his wife, who insisted he drop out."

"They must have some kind of secret," Lillie said. "I thought everyone who had magic was taken away. Or lives in Lower Pigsend."

"As I understand it, there are people who either slipped through the cracks or didn't have enough magic to be concerned with." Bev nodded to the front door. "Fernley, Allen's mother, had a little bit of pobyd magic, but only enough to enhance the flavors of her baked goods."

"Kinda like what Allen has now, hm?" Lillie touched her chin thoughtfully. "Everyone else has gone back to normal, right?"

"I believe so. At least, no one's acting strangely," Bev said. "Why?"

"I wonder if someone else out there still has their magic…activated, I guess I should say. Like Allen." Lillie said. "Like maybe the solstice woke it up, and now they've still got it."

"But why would that mean they'd want to threaten Pip and…" Bev caught herself in time. "Holly."

"I haven't a clue. Trying to look at it from all angles," Lillie said. "Have you looked into Freddie yet? I know everyone thinks Wilda's the worst because her cousin's the Middleburg mayor, but—"

"I have." Bev cleared her throat. She'd already let the cat out of the bag about Pip's letter to Lillie, but she wanted to keep Hans's letter a secret. "Not quite off the list, but not at the top of it, either."

"And Hendry?" Lillie asked.

"Something in my gut tells me it's not her," Bev said, unwilling to share her convoluted reasoning, lest another person find her mad. "But I'm keeping an open mind."

"So…Wilda," Lillie said with a bit of a pout. "That hardly seems fair, does it? Hendry's the one with the most to gain."

Bev held up her hands. "I'm not saying she did it, just that I currently don't have any evidence against it. Unless you have something?"

Lillie relaxed a little. "I wish I did, but I've been stuck baking. I've barely had a chance to talk with her at all."

"Who's running her campaign?" Bev asked. "Maybe I could chat with them?"

"She's running it herself, but I hear her cousin's going to come visit in a few days," Lillie said. "Obviously, Miranda won her election several times, so she's going to give some advice."

"Hendry won't like that," Bev said.

"Why?"

"Oh, that's right, you weren't around during the Harvest Festival," Bev said with a laugh. "Well, apart from a soldier masquerading as a judge who was destroying everyone's baked goods with magic, the Middleburg team, including, as I remember, Wilda, had gotten some magical baubles and were using them to bake with. Cheating."

Lillie gasped. "No."

"It was all part of an elaborate scheme to get Petula to move the Harvest Festival to Middleburg. Obviously, it failed, as we're having it here in a few months." Bev shrugged. "But Wilda was quite scarce from then on out."

"I can imagine. And now she's running for mayor?" Lillie let out a breath. "Guess people have short memories."

"Or they don't really care about the festival," Bev said. "In any case, I was going to hang around

Wilda's campaign today, see what I could find out. What's she up to?"

"Today?" Lillie thought for a moment. "She's going to be at her house this morning, practicing for the question-and-answer session this evening. She's put in an order for three dozen cupcakes that I've got to get going on, because she'll be taking them to all the voters who said they were undecided." She tapped her chin. "Then at six, they're doing the session in the town square, I think."

"What all does that entail?" Bev asked.

"From what I understand, Petula's going to put the candidates in different spots around the town square, and voters can walk up to them and ask questions," Lillie said. "It's supposed to be three hours, I think."

"Any question?" Bev asked. "Any voter? Seems like it would be a little haphazard."

"It works quite well." Petula's voice rang out from the landing. She walked down the stairs, once again wearing an impeccably crisp shirt and shined shoes, along with the large election monitor pin, although she, too, seemed like she could've slept longer. She also carried her thick rules and regulations book, along with a notepad, which she placed on the counter. She smiled at Lillie and Bev in greeting, and the latter offered her a muffin.

"Thank you," Petula said. "And did I also hear the kettle on earlier? Last night was long. Mr. Silver does live quite a way out from everywhere, doesn't he?"

"You certainly are making the rounds," Bev said. "Did you hear all the campaign speeches last night?"

She shook her head. "I unfortunately missed Ms. Murtagh's speech. But I do hope to spend some time with her today, listening to her answers and such. One of the unfortunate downsides of being a single person monitoring an election of this size."

"Is it normal for you to be running around like this?" Bev asked.

"Well, this election is a *bit* more widespread than anticipated." She cleared her throat, perhaps trying to choose her words carefully. "I was *unaware* that more than one candidate was running. When I wrote to Mayor Hendry a few weeks ago, she'd indicated it would be an uncontested election."

Lillie shot Bev a sideways look, but Bev kept Petula's gaze. "I'm sure she thought that would be the case."

"Yes, well, it's unfortunate that Mr. Norris decided to drop out, but it does make my job a little easier." Petula took a second muffin and placed it atop the book as she checked the clock. "Now, I do need to get going, but...how about that spot of tea?"

"Coming right up." Bev turned to Lillie. "Do you want one, too?"

"I've got to get back to the bakery, but..." Lillie

grinned. "I can wait a few minutes longer."

~

Bev made their tea, which Lillie took across the street and Petula enjoyed with her muffin. But there was a mountain of dishes waiting to be washed, and Bev had to make preparations for dinner. The crate of produce Hendry had brought had been used the night before, which meant Bev would have to make a trip to the market.

She headed back through the kitchen to the front room where Petula was still sipping her tea and reading through the rules and regulations book. Bev was sure Petula had read the thing front to back, and perhaps had sections of it memorized. At least, that's how it was with the Harvest Festival. Perhaps the monitor was lacking something interesting to read.

"We do have a library in town," Bev said, as she rapped on the door. "If you'd like something less dry to read. Max has a few fiction titles, though perhaps not as many as you'd find in Queen's Capital."

"Oh, I'm fine. Nice to brush up on details, you know." She tittered. "This tea is hitting the spot, though. What kind of blend is it?"

"It's one of Etheldra's," Bev said. "She's an ornery old cur, but she can make a delicious cup of tea."

"Indeed, she can." Petula toyed with the corner of the paper. "I see she and Mr. Dollman got married. That's lovely."

"We all thought so, too." Bev walked farther into the room, remembering she'd come in here for a reason. "What time does this question-and-answer session start this evening?"

"It begins around six," Petula said.

Bev made a thoughtful noise, tapping her finger to her chin. "Maybe I'll push dinner up to five-thirty again. I'm sure there will be more than a few people passing through, and I'd like to see some of the session myself."

"Sounds good, dear," Petula said absently as she returned to the book. She was reading a section on the question-and-answer event, which Bev supposed it made sense to brush up on the particulars.

"How long have you been doing elections?" Bev asked.

"Six months. But as I said, that's what I used to do before I was, erm." She cleared her throat and closed the book. "Six months. It's quite a passion of mine, you know. I'm so thrilled the queen takes local elections as seriously as she takes everything else."

"And you said you weren't expecting there to be this many candidates," Bev said.

"A robust competition never hurt anyone. Except my aching feet." She smiled brightly. "But that's all part and parcel of the job, you know. Happy to see so many people engaged in civic matters. Warms my heart."

"How does one go from elections to Harvest Festivals and back again?" Bev asked. "If you don't mind me asking?"

Based on the flush that crept up Petula's cheeks, she very much *did* mind Bev asking. "Just a bit of a misunderstanding. That's why my stint in Harvest Festivals was so short, you know. Just needed to earn back a bit of trust before I could be given such an important task." She stood and fiddled with her book and papers, avoiding Bev's gaze. "It was all so silly, really. And I did enjoy the Harvest Festivals. Goodness knows tasting pies and jams and bread wasn't the worst job in the world."

"I bet not," Bev said. "And you were quite good at it. No funny business on your watch."

"Indeed not," Petula said. "Your Harvest Festival was the only such calamity, and I made sure to raise Mr. Renault and his perfidy up the flagpole."

Bev started, remembering Petula had had an escort with her during the festival. "What happened to the soldiers who came with you last year?"

"Hm?" Petula laughed. "Well, I daresay they've been assigned to another festival monitor."

"Yes, but," Bev furrowed her brow, "it's a bit strange that you had a pair of soldiers escorting you at the Harvest Festival, which doesn't really matter in the grand scheme of things. But now, you're here by yourself for this local election. Surely, *this* merits some kind of additional oversight by Her Majesty's forces—"

The blush was now all the way up Petula's face. "Look at the time! I must get going. Lots to do today. Thank you so much for the mea and the tuffins—er, tea and muffins." She laughed as she scooped up her book. "Ta-ta, Bev. I'm sure I'll see you around town."

The door shut before Bev could even wish her farewell, and Bev eyed it suspiciously. Biscuit, who'd been waiting patiently for one of Lillie's muffins, walked to the door and sniffed it.

"You thought that was dodgy, too, hm?" Bev said, looking around. "Maybe we have a third suspect. Or, at least, perhaps another reason for the letters."

Biscuit whined, tilting his head.

"Well, I don't know how they would know about PJ or Hans," Bev said, throwing her hands up. "That's why this one's a puzzler." She stopped, eyeing him. "*You* can't suddenly talk, can you? Blabbing secrets all over town?"

He sneezed, as if he'd inhaled some pepper.

"I told you. I'm stumped," Bev said with a sigh. "Looking at all the possible angles. But I'm curious why Her Majesty thought sending a pair of soldiers to a Harvest Festival made more sense than sending them to help with a local election."

Biscuit sniffed.

Chapter Ten

Unfortunately, if Bev wanted to discover Petula's secrets, she'd have to travel all the way to Queen's Capital, so that thread would have to wait. Instead, Bev finished her chores and headed across the street to the butcher shop. Ida was there, continuing the trend of looking quite tired, but perked up as soon as Bev walked in.

"Morning, you!" Ida cheered. "What a night last night, eh? The band played until at least two. Vellora insisted I dance the night with her, but then *whined* this morning that it was too early. So here I am, manning the shop." Ida snorted. "She'd better allow me a nap later, that's all I'm saying."

"You can join Lillie at the inn," Bev said. "I hear

Wilda's keeping her up all hours of the night with parties, too."

"Wilda." Ida glowered. "Why doesn't she do us all a favor and drop out? Who in their right mind is supporting *her*?"

Bev listed a few people, and Ida waved her off when she mentioned the bakers. "Oh, Lillie's saying that because she lives there. And Allen's friends with Lillie. Neither of them really thinks she'd make a good mayor, do they?"

Bev didn't feel like getting sucked into another argument about who supported whom, so she put in her order, wished Ida a good day, and left the butcher shop.

Knowing the bakers were as busy as she was, Bev popped over to see if they needed anything from the market. Inside, Lillie and Allen were hard at work, with Lillie carefully icing her three dozen cupcakes. When Bev walked in, her face fell.

"I thought you might be coming to bring me another cup."

"Sorry," Bev said. "I can run across the street if you like?"

"No, no. It's fine." She sighed, looking at the cupcakes before bending down to continue icing them. "I've just got to get these finished, then I think I can take a break."

"I'm headed to the farmers' market," Bev said. "Do you need anything? I don't have my wagon, but I can probably grab a few extra things."

"We're full up here, but thanks, Bev," Allen said. "The root cellar's still bursting with berries and stone fruits."

"And lucky for us, Wilda's determined for us to use all of it," Lillie said with a smirk.

"I do hope you're getting paid for all this work," Bev said.

"Yes, of course," Allen said. "Though I have to admit, I think Wilda's asking a *bit* too much of us. We do have other customers to consider, and we've got a slew of pies and cakes ordered. As soon as these come out of the oven, I've got to head up to Petra Reyfield's house to deliver them. It'll take me near an hour to get there and back."

"Doesn't she live near Middleburg?" Bev asked.

Allen smiled proudly. "She does. Said ours was better and decided to buy her weekly pie from us. It's a bit of a hassle, really, but she's paying us for our trouble, and she's already requested a five-tier birthday cake in the same flavor as my wedding cake in two months, so I'd like to keep her happy."

Bev beamed at the two of them. "Well, I'm glad you didn't take Mr. Abora up on his offer then, Lillie."

Allen frowned. "What offer?"

"Oh, I didn't tell you?" Lillie put her hand to her head. "I'd almost forgotten about it, to be honest. During the solstice, one of Bev's guests was in town looking for people to move to a small city south of here. Silverkeep, I think it was?"

"Why?" Allen asked.

"Apparently, the queen cleared out most of their people," Bev said. "The mayor wanted Kemp to scour the countryside and find people interested in setting up shop. He asked Lillie, but she declined."

"Aw." Allen smiled at her. "You could've gone, you know. If you wanted."

"I told him it's a not-now, not a not-ever," Lillie said. "Besides that, I knew what we had on the schedule. How poor a friend would I be if I left you in the lurch like that?"

"His visit wasn't for nothing, though. He did snatch Gilda from Gore," Bev said with a laugh. "Gore isn't too pleased about that, from what I understand. But if he wanted her to stick around, he should've made her a partner and not an apprentice. Etheldra, at least, had the sense to offer the same to Shasta."

"Right, she was telling me about that," Lillie said. "Etheldra's going to retire next year, right?"

"So she says, but we'll see," Bev said. Etheldra might follow in Rosie Kelooke's footsteps and never *quite* feel happy leaving her life's work in someone else's hands. "Those do look lovely, Lillie. I know Wilda will be happy."

Lillie smiled as she placed a single candied lemon peel atop each one.

As if summoned, Wilda strode by the window and opened the front door. "Good morning, good morning to my favorite bakers!" Her voice echoed in the space, like Hendry's always did. "Look at you two. Working away. Warms my heart to see you so busy."

"I'm about finished, Wilda," Lillie said, carefully placing another lemon peel. "Then they're all yours."

"Mine?" She tittered. "My dear Lillie, I was hoping you'd go with me. After all, it's so warm, the icing will melt if left in the sun too long."

Bev didn't understand, but Lillie's frown deepened. "I'm sorry?"

"Come, come, we all know you've got a little extra *something*," Wilda said with a wink. "I don't think it's a surprise to anyone here, is it? Certainly not to me, who lives with you."

Lillie swallowed with a half-smile. "S-suppose not. But I can't leave the bakery. Allen's got to make a delivery and—"

"Why don't I go with you, Wilda?" Bev cut in before Lillie could answer. "After all, Lillie and Allen *do* have a lot of work. And I can help you deliver these before they melt, too."

"I thought you were going to the farmers' market," Allen said with a frown.

"Oh, that's fine, I'm headed in that direction anyway." Wilda turned to Bev, a smile forming on her face. "Does this mean I can count on your vote?"

Bev returned her smile. "I'm not telling *anyone* who I'm voting for. But my dear friends need a little assistance, so I'm happy to help them."

And she was even happier to have some time with her prime suspect.

~

Wilda didn't seem bothered by Bev's lack of commitment to voting for her. She and Hendry were more alike than Bev had thought, especially as Wilda made no move to take the cupcake tray from Bev. She marched purposefully to the west, humming to herself and keeping a brisk pace as they left Pigsend behind in favor of the farmlands.

She didn't say anything, which gave Bev time to consider her plan of attack. Not to say Wilda's knowledge of Lillie meant she'd written the letters, especially as they lived together, but it did strike Bev as odd that she'd bring it up now. Almost like the candidate was in a blackmail sort of mood.

"Keep up, Bev. We've got a lot of ground to cover today," Wilda called as Bev fell a little behind.

"And to whom are we delivering these?" Bev asked, doing her best to keep an eye on the road for tripping hazards while also balancing the cupcakes so they wouldn't touch. "And why?"

"I'm sure it's *no* surprise to you that I've got ground to make up with the folks who live outside

Pigsend proper. The farmers, they say, have all banded to Freddie's side, but I'm not one to give up easily. I've picked a few I *think* could be swayed."

"You're going to bribe them with cupcakes?" Bev asked with a quirked brow.

"Not *bribe*, my dear Bev. I'm going to *invite* them to the question-and-answer session tonight and ask that they come hear what I have to say. The cupcake's merely a gift." She smiled, as if there was a difference between what she was describing and a bribe. "Obviously."

"Obviously, yeah." Bev spotted a root up ahead and made sure to step over it. "So, erm, how long have you known Lillie was…different?"

Bev didn't want to come out and say the word *pobyd*. She wasn't exactly sure how much Wilda knew about where Lillie came from and what she was, so she didn't want to volunteer anything.

"Initially, I thought she was just an outstanding baker." Wilda said. "And it would be fun to have someone so skilled living with me. Thought perhaps I could pick up on a few things. You know, I'm quite the pie-maker myself."

Bev swallowed her comment about Wilda cheating in the pie-making contest with a magical bauble the year before.

"Then, during the solstice when *everything* was going higgledy-piggledy and the bread on my counter began dancing whenever she walked into the room, I figured it out. Can't say I'm *too* upset. Might give me the edge I've been looking for with the judges at the Harvest Festival."

Bev had to keep herself from narrowing her gaze. "You'd want Lillie to use her magic to help you win?"

"Oh, no, no. Of *course* not." Wilda laughed like she hadn't tried the exact same thing the year before. "Lillie's skill is much more than her magic, dear Bev. She's got a keen palate, and her artistry's unmatched. I mean, look at that lemon peel!" She gestured to the cupcakes. "Allen, bless him, is quite good, but he lacks that artistic eye."

Bev didn't disagree with that statement. "I'm not sure passing Lillie's baking off as yours is—"

"I would do the baking, of course. I'd ask her to…well, help me with the flourishes." Wilda smiled as she turned to Bev. "Now, the better question is: how do *you* know what Lillie is?"

Bev stumbled and only barely recovered the cupcakes before they all landed in the dirt. She hadn't been expecting that question. "Oh, um." She swallowed. "Well, I suppose…that…I, too, had my suspicions when she stayed at the inn. One night, I asked her about it, and she confided in me."

"Mm. And she hasn't been, erm, *helping* with the rosemary bread I always hear rave reviews about?"

"Of course not," Bev snapped, a little more

harshly than she'd meant to. But she *did* pride herself in tending to her bread all by herself. "The only thing Lillie's done for my bread was suggest I could proof it in my root cellar overnight. But that was a suggestion—"

"That's *all* I'm asking of her, too," Wilda said, smiling as if she'd proven a point.

Bev was about to ask if she knew of anyone else in town with magical secrets—perhaps getting her closer to revealing she wrote the letter—but Wilda abruptly turned off the road and strode down a dirt pathway between two sets of fallow fields. Bev recognized the house as Bathilda Wormwood's and winced.

"Not sure Bathilda's going to want to see us today," Bev said, catching up with Wilda.

"Why not? I come bearing cupcakes."

"Yes, but…" If Bathilda had a unicorn or griffon or some other kind of magical creature hidden in her house, she might meet the candidate with a crossbow, as she'd once done to Bev.

Wilda rapped on the door and stood back, smiling.

Bev swallowed, hoping the farmer-turned-magical-creature-dealer hadn't taken in anything new and interesting.

When no one answered, Wilda knocked again. "Bathilda, dear? It's Wilda Murtagh and Bev… erm…Bev from the Weary Dragon. Are you home, love?"

The sound of footsteps echoed from the other side of the door, which swung open, revealing Bathilda's grumpy face. Her hair was growing back from where a phoenix had burned it off, and beyond her short frame, her living room still bore the scorch marks. But to Bev's eyes, there didn't seem to be another creature in the house. Perhaps Bathilda had finally learned her lesson.

"Yeah? Whatdya want?" Bathilda grumbled, looking at Bev curiously.

Bev turned to Wilda, who was waiting for Bev to speak. When Bev didn't, Wilda cleared her throat. "Well, Bathilda, I couldn't help but notice you *weren't* at the candidate announcement the other night, nor have you been to any of the events —"

"Yeah, what of it?"

Bev was a bit surprised Wilda knew who was at the other candidates' events. Had she sent one of her campaign people to check? "I was hoping to invite you to the question-and-answer session tonight," Wilda continued, undeterred, plucking one of the cupcakes off the tray. "And I also wanted to give you one of these beautiful cupcakes. The bakers—Allen and Lillie—made a surplus of them and asked me to take them around town."

"Sure. I'll take one." Bathilda snatched the pastry from her hand and took a big bite. "But I ain't coming to your election nonsense. Don't care who the mayor is. Doesn't affect me one bit."

"But—"

Bathilda slammed the door in her face.

"She's certainly taken a turn for the worse," Bev muttered. But she wasn't surprised. Bathilda's newfound career of dealing in illegal creatures meant she probably wanted to avoid anything to do with politics, the queen, or her laws. "Well, where to next?"

Wilda's next stop was the farmers' market, which actually suited Bev fine, because she could pick up a few things for dinner that evening, assuming she could hand the cupcakes off to Wilda and get back to the inn. Much like the bakers, Bev couldn't devote her entire day to helping Wilda, as much as she'd been hoping to see something revealing.

But the candidate scowled as she approached the market, as there was already a small crowd around Freddie. Vellora stood next to him, holding a plate of sausages and beaming, while Gore stood off to the side, handing out small napkins and talking to the farmers.

"Maybe we should—" Bev started, but Wilda marched headfirst toward the crowd.

Freddie stopped mid-sentence and stared at her, earning the curiosity of the others gathered in the space. "Wilda, what in the world are you doing here? And what are those?"

"Cupcakes, my dear Freddie," Wilda said. "And I could ask you the same question. What are you doing here in the market? It's not time for an official campaign event. I'd hate to have to report you to Petula."

Bev turned to her, surprised. "What do you mean?"

"Per that thick, *detailed* book of Petula's, candidates are only allowed to conduct official events at designated times unless otherwise authorized by the election monitor," Wilda said with a knowing smile. "This sort of thing could disqualify you, Freddie."

"Yeah, and you'd know all about that, wouldn't you?" Gore said, marching forward. "Are you trying to buy votes with sweets?"

"Only if you're doing the same with sausage links," Wilda said. "But no, the bakers asked me to deliver cupcakes to Bathilda, but I think they got their wires crossed. She told us she hadn't ordered any, so here we are with a plate of delicious morsels and no one to enjoy them." She took the tray from Bev and wafted it in front of the nearest farmer. "Might I tempt you—"

"Don't touch 'em," Gore snarled, pointing his finger at Wilda. "Those came from the bakers, right? No telling what sort of nonsense they put in them."

"What makes you say that?" Bev asked, narrowing her gaze. "There's nothing in these cupcakes but sugar, flour, butter, and egg."

"Do I take your presence as a sign that you're voting for Wilda, Bev?" Gore asked.

"Lillie was swamped at the bakery, and Allen had a faraway delivery," Bev said. "I had some time to spare, and I also had to pick up some potatoes and other things for dinner." She crossed her arms. "What did you mean by *nonsense* put in the cupcakes?"

"He's being overzealous," Vellora said with a wave of her hand. "Ignore him. The cupcakes look great. I'm sure Lillie worked hard on them."

Wilda scowled as Vellora took one; clearly, the butcher wasn't going to be swayed to vote for someone else.

"Delicious," Vellora said. "Try one, everyone. After all, they did bring them all the way out here."

Bev saw through Vellora's kindness too late, and before she knew it, the entire tray of cupcakes was gone. Wilda's scowl deepened, but she couldn't say anything about it—even when Freddie took three.

"Hans does love sweets," he said. "Thank you, Wilda, for your generosity. Now, if you'll excuse me, I've got to get moving. Lots of ground to cover before the session this evening!"

Chapter Eleven

With no cupcakes remaining to deliver, a very disgruntled Wilda left right after that, saddling Bev with the empty tray. This election was starting to get too contentious—and that was in addition to the blackmail letters.

With Wilda gone, Freddie turned to the farmers to continue his stump speech, and Bev did her best to ignore what Wilda had said about illegal campaign events as she poked through the potatoes and grabbed a bunch of carrots. She was anticipating a crowd this evening, so a few more side dishes wouldn't hurt.

"You, erm, aren't going to tell Petula about this, are you?" Gore asked.

"Not planning on it," Bev said, picking up a few potatoes from Alice Estrich's stand. She made sure no one else was around before asking, "Has Freddie gotten any more letters?"

Gore let out a low breath. "Hans told you?"

Bev nodded. "He's not the only one who got one. I'm trying to figure out who sent them."

"Is that why you were with Wilda?" He frowned. "Did she get one, too?"

"Not that I'm aware of," Bev said.

"Well, I told Hans to burn it," Gore said. "We're not going to be bullied by some nameless, faceless person. Besides that, all Hans needs is a bit of your crumble, and he's right as rain, isn't he?"

"Yes, but—"

"I've put too much into this campaign to be put off by Wilda or Hendry or whoever's behind it," Gore said. "So if I were you, I'd let sleeping dogs lie. No harm, no foul, eh? Pip's out of the race, and it doesn't look like anyone else is dropping out."

"Is there anyone else who might know of Hans's powers?" Bev asked. "I'm trying to find a connection between Hans and Pip and—"

"They keep it close to the vest," Gore said. "Leave it alone, Bev." He pointed to the bags behind Alice's stand. "And you might want to buy extra. We've been telling our voters they can get dinner at the Weary Dragon tonight."

That would've been nice to know yesterday, when I

made the bread. "I see."

"Maybe a nice succulent beef roast, eh? I'm sure Vellora's got a large cut in the shop. Might be easiest to throw everything into a single pot and let it simmer, you know?"

"I assume you'll be going to my kitchen to start the fires?" Bev glanced at the sun—noon. It would cut it close, but if she headed back immediately, she could get it done. "Fine. I'll put on a roast."

"Excellent."

"But I still think—"

"Got to get a move on," Gore said, cutting her off. "Lots of ground to cover. Headed out to the farmers who signed their name to Hendry's campaign. I'm sure they didn't know there was an alternative, so we're off to inform them, while, of course, inviting them to the session tonight."

With that, he lumbered away, announcing to the farmers gathered that the candidate had a schedule to keep. Freddie and Gore climbed onto a waiting wagon. Vellora was about to get in herself, but after a brief conversation with Gore, in which some coin exchanged hands, Vellora stayed where she was until the wagon was down the street. Finally, when they'd passed over the first hill, she turned with a smile and walked over to Bev.

"I hear I'm to ensure you get a large cut of cow," Vellora said. "And don't worry, Freddie's already paid for it."

"I don't quite think that's fair," Bev said.

"Think of it as our apology for putting you out. I'd thought Gore had told you we were steering people to you, but apparently not." She gestured to Bev to walk with her. "Let's head back, and we'll get you squared away."

Bev paid for her potatoes and carrots, and Vellora offered to carry the heavy sack back for her. As a rule, Bev would've declined, but the bag was bulky, and even though she lacked her wife's super strength, Vellora was still much more capable of carrying things than Bev was.

"Gore's certainly intent on Freddie winning, isn't he?" Bev asked Vellora.

"Yeah." She smiled at Bev, and it was almost a little too friendly. "I hope he wasn't too rude to you. He's been on a bit of a tear lately."

"Nothing I can't handle," Bev said.

"But seriously…are you voting for Wilda?" Vellora asked in a hushed tone.

"I don't know who I'm voting for," Bev said. "Might vote for Hendry out of pity."

Vellora looked stricken.

"Kidding," Bev said with a laugh. "But I'd tell your candidate's campaign manager to ease up a bit, huh? Most folks in town don't care too much about who the mayor is."

"That's where you're wrong, Bev," Vellora said. "I advise you to think long and hard about your choice. We only get one shot at this every few years, and the choice this time is the most important of our lifetimes."

"Vellora, it's Pigsend." Bev laughed but Vellora didn't join in, so she quickly changed the subject.

~

Their paths diverged in front of the inn, with Vellora headed to the shop to retrieve the beef, and Bev going to stoke the fires at the inn. While that was warming up, she headed to the bakery to bring Lillie's empty cupcake platter back to her. Lillie was icing a child's birthday cake, complete with small fireworks, and smiled when Bev walked in.

"That was fast," Lillie said. "I thought Wilda would've still been wandering the countryside."

Bev told her about running into Freddie, and how he and his team had descended on the sweets. Bev found it amusing, but based on Lillie's growing frown, the baker did not.

"I spent ages on those stupid things," Lillie said. "I'd hoped they would've at least gone to an undecided voter or two."

"Bathilda's undecided," Bev said, conveniently leaving out that Bathilda probably wouldn't be voting for anyone to spare Lillie's feelings. "She had one and enjoyed it immensely."

Lillie heartened a little. "Well, suppose I'll have another crack at the population at large this evening."

"Don't tell me—"

"More cupcakes, yes. And…" She smiled at Bev bashfully. "Wilda wants me to bake a cake to be served at the inn this evening. Apparently, she's been telling people to get a meal at the Weary Dragon before the session tonight."

"Uh-huh." Bev might not have enough seats. "And that cake's already paid for?"

Lillie half-smiled. "Yeah."

"Freddie's paid for my meat, too," Bev said. "Next thing you know, Hendry will be in here, kneading my bread dough."

"Oh, don't you dare let her do that," Lillie said with a chuckle. "She doesn't have the *technique*."

"Suppose the election is good for business, in any case," Bev said. She glanced out the window, where Vellora was carrying a large cut of beef. "Lillie, aren't you a little worried Wilda knew about your powers? Did you have any clue?"

"She'd never mentioned it," Lillie said. "But I can't say it's all that surprising, you know? We do live together." She paused, eyeing Bev. "You don't think she's the one who…?"

"I don't know what I think," Bev said. "If Freddie hadn't *also* received a letter, I'd suspect him, too. Or Gore. But Wilda telling you to use magic in your cupcakes, that was concerning."

"She's never said anything like that to me," Lillie said. "Up until now, everything we've done for the campaign has been bought and paid for, or she's prorated my rent." She leaned in, as if Wilda would overhear their conversation if she spoke too loudly. "Don't tell her, but I put a time limit on the magic. Dissipated in an hour, so probably a good thing you ran into Freddie, because they might not have lasted much longer."

"I'm glad for that," Bev said. "And you still don't think she's the one blackmailing Pip, asking you to stick your neck out like that?"

Lillie opened and closed her mouth, clearly unable to come up with a retort.

So Bev saved her. "Are you headed to the question-and-answer session?"

"Another thing I'm *expected* to help with," Lillie said with an eye roll. "As soon as Allen gets back, I'm headed home to nap so I can be refreshed. Wilda might tell the town who I am if I don't come support her. I haven't told her I'm not allowed to cast a vote at all."

"Why are you expected to help with tonight? Surely, Wilda will be doing most of the work."

"Oh, *no*, Bev," Lillie said dramatically. "Everyone in the campaign has been given a list of questions to ask her."

"Isn't the point of this so undecided voters can ask questions?" Bev asked.

"You'd think, but no. Wilda says that leaves too much up to chance." Lillie turned the cake as she inspected it. "So she's got me, the twins, Allen, and her brother Lazlo queued up with questions to ask her. We're supposed to rotate, too, so every hour, we're back asking her the same questions, so people who came later can hear."

"That doesn't seem to give anyone else a chance to ask her anything," Bev said.

"No. But I think that's the point."

~

Bev had dinner to make, so she returned to her hot kitchen. Vellora had taken the liberty of putting the meat in a pan and sticking it in the oven, but had failed to add any aromatics, so Bev carefully pulled the pan from the hot oven and added some onions, a few rough chopped carrots, and some herbs. Then she set to her potatoes and the rest of her carrots, peeling and thinking about the day's events.

Her thoughts mostly centered on Wilda, who was acting more like Mayor Hendry than anyone except the good mayor herself. She knew exactly what was expected of her and was doing *enough* to meet the letter of the rules but not the intent. Bev didn't doubt she'd tell Petula about Freddie's campaign event if she thought it would give her a leg up. And her story changed with every new conversation.

But did that mean she was the guilty one or was she being the quintessential politician?

And then Gore, too, was almost *too* invested in Freddie's campaign for someone whose name wasn't on the ballot. Bev hadn't been able to get a minute alone with Freddie to see if he shared his manager's zealousness. But then again, could she really consider Freddie a suspect when his own husband had been the recipient of a nasty letter, and Gore had been the one to bury it?

Then there was Hendry, who Bev hadn't seen all day but was presumably still in the race. Could all this trouble have come from her?

"More questions, few answers," Bev said to Biscuit as she tossed him a potato skin, which he gobbled up. "At least there's nothing magical afoot, eh? Nice to have a couple days where something's not destroying the town."

Biscuit ruffed, almost as if to warn her against jinxing herself.

Dinner was ready around five-thirty, and as Bev brought out the first plate, she was glad Vellora had delivered such a big cut of meat and Allen had delivered a three-tier cherry-and-vanilla cake. There was room for eighteen at three tables, and Bev counted at least twenty-five standing around. Mostly farmers from out of town, but Max, Bardoff, Earl, and Etheldra were there as well, already queued up with plates in hand, as if worried they wouldn't get fed.

"Harrumph." Etheldra snorted as she looked

around at those gathered. "Hope you made enough."

"I had a feeling it would be busy," Bev said, gesturing to the platters full of succulent beef and potatoes in front of them. "There should be plenty for everybody."

Etheldra certainly didn't seem to think so as she piled food onto her plate and took an extra slice of bread. Earl, right behind her, served himself a normal amount as he smiled a bit forlornly.

"How are you today, Earl?" Bev asked. "Pip and Holly all right?"

"Yeah, yeah," he said with a sad sigh. "Tried to change his mind about dropping out until I was blue in the face, but he said he'd already told Petula to cross out his name. Won't even be appearing at the question-and-answer session this evening."

Bev tutted. "I can imagine it might be a sore subject for him."

"Yeah, but..." He grunted. "Now who am I gonna vote for? Freddie? He's too young. Got too many ideas. Wilda? She's got the stink of—"

"Middleburg," Bev finished, having heard that refrain before. "There's also Hendry."

He shook his head, as if she were the *most* awful of the three. "We'll see what happens tonight."

He joined his wife at one of the tables, and Bev turned her attention to the next person in line. Mandy Nowak lived east of town, usually only coming in for the Harvest Festival, and was a bit unsure what to do when it was her turn to serve herself.

"Beef, from the Witzels next door, potatoes, and some carrots, too," Bev said, pointing to each plate. "Take as much as you like."

"But not too much!" Etheldra called.

"She's got ears like a bat," Mandy said, rubbing the back of her head. She only took a small amount, and half a slice of bread.

"Which candidate are you going to listen to?" Bev asked.

"Oh, I'm sure I'll rotate around to all of 'em," she said. "Freddie, being a farmer, might get my vote, but he's a bit too..." She made a face. "Some of his ideas are good, but some of 'em seem to come outta nowhere. Bit of fantasy land, you know?"

Bev nodded. "Wilda?"

She sighed. "She's too much like Hendry. Politician through and through. But like I said, I don't know who I'm going to vote for until I get there."

Bev could appreciate that and heard much the same from the others in line who served themselves. Everyone except Etheldra had been judicious with their servings, and while several farmers had to sit on the stairs going up to the inn, and others juggled their ale tankards and plates while they stood along the walls, everyone was served. Bev had enough food, plates, and tankards for everyone, though she was scraping the bottom of the bowls to do so. The cake, too, was divvied up completely and shared, and Bev had to admit, it was one of Allen's better creations.

Unfortunately, with all the food eaten, Biscuit, who usually enjoyed the inn's leftovers, would go hungry that night—although he'd eaten his weight in potato skins earlier, so she didn't feel too bad about it.

"I'll find you something in the root cellar," Bev promised him, patting him on the head. "After the campaign event."

"I'm sure he'll find something at the question session," Earl said, bringing his empty plate to Bev. "I hear the Witzels are going to be bringing more grilled meat, and Allen and Lillie have some pastries, too."

"Sweet versus savory," Bev said with a shake of her head. "The battle of Pigsend stomachs continues."

"One has to feel for poor Hendry, though," Bardoff said, coming with his plate. "I can't believe she's still in the race. I haven't found a single person to vote for her."

"Don't feel *too* bad," Earl said. "I'm sure she'll come up with a sneaky way to get herself into first or second place. It happens every election, you know?"

Bev glanced at the clock and cleared her throat. "It's getting close to six, everyone. If you're done, bring me your plates and I'll get them in the kitchen."

Chapter Twelve

The diners stuffed the last bits of beef and rosemary bread into their mouths and did as Bev asked, and before long, she and the group were making their way down to the town square. Unlike the other events, which were inside the town hall, Petula had wanted an open space to accommodate a large crowd that could move freely.

Wilda had been stationed near the library, and her voice carried as she welcomed everyone who stood nearby, whether they wanted to be in her area or not. Wilda's brother Lazlo, Allen, and Shasta were already standing there at the ready.

Freddie and his cohort had been stationed over near the schoolhouse, standing on the same stage

Bev had seen constructed at his home. Bev didn't see anyone ready to ask questions, though Ida, Vellora, and Gore were working the crowd in the middle, trying to get them to meander over to Freddie's corner.

In front of the town hall, perhaps by design, was Hendry. She stood on the front steps, gazing out at the crowd with her arms crossed. She had no contingent or campaign workers, nor did she have a crowd gathered to ask her questions. Bev had to imagine everyone in town had already asked her all they needed to.

The busiest person, however, was Petula, who was flitting from corner to corner with a pencil and paper on her clipboard, trying to be in three places at once. She'd listen to Wilda's questions, then head over to Freddie to hear his answers. Every so often, she'd pause in front of Hendry, but as no one was conversing with the mayor, there was no need to stop and listen. So back she went.

"She's an odd creature, isn't she?" Etheldra asked, coming to stand next to Bev. "Thought she was uppity during the Harvest Festival, but this seems to take things to a new level."

Bev nodded. "You remember she had those soldiers with her at the festival?"

"Vaguely. I don't make a habit of remembering which of Her Majesty's forces come into town."

"I was asking her why they'd accompanied her

to that and not to this," Bev said. "She didn't give me an answer."

Etheldra eyed her. "Is there some kind of conspiracy afoot, Bev? Because if so, you'll have to enlighten me." Her gaze narrowed. "Did someone pressure Pip to drop out?"

"My lips are sealed," Bev said.

"Say no more." Etheldra gazed at the crowd as if seeing them in a new light. "I'm on it."

What, exactly, *it* was, Bev didn't know, but Etheldra moved through the crowd as if she were Biscuit on the scent of something juicy or magical. Bev watched her for a moment, amused, then realized she needed to be making her own rounds.

Out of curiosity, Bev went to Freddie's station first, where he was half-finished with a long-winded explanation of how he planned to tackle the new rules and regulations around wheat harvesting. The question had come from one of the diners at the inn, and he was nodding approvingly. Perhaps Freddie had won one over.

"How was dinner?" Gore asked, coming to stand next to Bev. "I heard it was a busy crowd."

"It was," Bev said. "Thank you for telling me what to expect. Though, I don't know if you knew, but I make my bread the night before, so we didn't have quite enough for everyone."

He nodded. "Breadmaking is a science I don't want to think about. Better to keep my hands on iron and ore, you know?"

Bev looked at the crowd. "Are you able to manage your shop with being campaign manager, too? Especially with Gilda gone?"

"I've got a few orders waiting an extra day or so," he said. "Including, unfortunately, fixing your wagon wheel. But I'm finding it hard to sleep, so I do a lot of my work in the early morning hours. Much cooler then, too."

"I can appreciate that," Bev said. "Is, erm, my wagon wheel going to be fixed any time soon?"

"Depends on if I can count on your vote."

Ida passed by with a large tray full of individually portioned pieces of sausage on skewers, offering a taste to everyone who was hungry.

"I can't remember when an election was so... labor intensive," Bev said instead of answering Gore's question.

"Well, you don't remember anything before five years ago, eh?" Gore said. "If you'll excuse me, I need to chat with Charles over there."

He left her standing there, crossing the crowd to meet a farmer who'd rounded the corner. He waved at Gore as if they were old friends and patted the blacksmith on the back. But instead of coming closer into the crowd, they turned to walk out of it.

"Bev!" Ida flashed a pan of sausage in front of her face. "Can I tempt you?"

"I'm full, thanks, but I know someone who's

always hungry." Bev nodded to Biscuit, who was sitting by her feet.

He unfurled his tongue to Ida, and she scowled, much as Lillie had when she'd heard Freddie had eaten her cupcakes.

"Fine." Ida tossed one down.

"Mind the skew—" Bev said, but Biscuit gobbled the sausage piece up in a second, snapping the skewer between his strong teeth. "Well, hopefully that passes fine."

"He's got a strong stomach," Ida said, a little remorsefully pulling the skewer out before tossing another piece on the ground.

Freddie had moved on to discussing how he was planning to fight the new livestock restrictions Her Majesty had passed down recently. But midway through his discussion, there was a loud question from the back.

"And how, exactly, do you plan on doing that?" The person who'd spoken was a farmer Bev hadn't ever seen before, and she wasn't quite sure they were *from* Pigsend.

Freddie cleared his throat, looking around for Gore, but when he didn't see his manager, he cleared his throat awkwardly. "Well, I plan to petition the regional governor," he said, after a moment. "Travel to his city to speak to him one-on-one—"

"Who are you, anyway?" Vellora asked, coming

to stand next to Freddie. "I've never seen you before."

He lifted a shoulder. "I live south of here. But this guy hasn't answered my question. How is he, a mayor from a small town, going to petition the queen, who by my recollection, isn't really in the mood to listen to anyone?"

"I think he told you," Vellora said, narrowing her gaze. "He's going to travel—"

"I want to hear from him, not you." The man crossed his arms over his chest. "Or is the candidate too scared to speak?"

Freddie once again went into a monologue about his plans to affect change, but the man wasn't convinced, peppering him with questions and demanding better answers.

"Erm, excuse me," Petula said, coming up to tap him on the shoulder. "Ms. Witzel informed me that you aren't familiar. This event is restricted to eligible voting citizens of Pigsend, so if you'll give me your name and where you live, I'd be happy to confirm."

He scowled and gave her a name and location, and she nodded and headed off, presumably to check it in Max's large book. But the man, perhaps scared off, took the break in the conversation, stuffed his hands in his pockets and left Freddie's gaggle.

Bev, intrigued, followed behind, keeping her distance. He bypassed Hendry, who'd sat on the front steps, and headed straight to Wilda's side of the square.

Wilda was mid-conversation with someone, talking about how she was the candidate with the most preparation *and* desire for change, which obviously set her apart. Bev stood ten paces from the man, who listened intently for a few minutes. Bev thought that might be all he would do, but as soon as there was a break in the questions, he spoke up.

"I gotta ask, your cousin's from Middleburg, yeah?" His voice was loud and carried across the crowd.

"Uh, yes, but I'm actually answering questions from this citizen right now," Wilda said, pointing to Lillie.

The man smirked. "She can't ask you. She ain't from Pigsend. Can't vote, can't ask questions."

"She lives with me," Wilda said.

"She moved here four months ago, didn't she? Ain't eligible," he said. "In any case, my question to you is how do you expect us to vote for you when you're obviously being influenced by the Middleburg mayor?"

"That's a preposterous question," Wilda said. "And I'm not answering it."

"You have to," he pressed. "That's what this is, isn't it? Questions and answers. And I asked you a question, so you gotta answer."

Wilda's cheeks reddened as she fumbled over her

words, clearly why she'd meant to have *only* pre-planned questions—though Bev didn't think it was quite fair to the rest of the town.

"My cousin is simply that—a cousin. She's offered her advice on running a campaign, but she's not..." She cleared her throat. "I'm my own person."

"A likely story. You're the one who helped the Middleburg people cheat at the Harvest Festival, ain't you?"

Now Wilda's face was beet red. "I didn't *cheat*, young man."

"You used magic, and—"

"I'm sorry, but who are you?" Bev asked, her curiosity getting the better of her. "I've never seen you around town before."

"I live on the outskirts," he said. "And you'd better get back to your breadmaking, if you know what's good for you."

"Bread—" Bev's eyebrows rose. "How did you know I own the Weary Dragon?"

Wilda had taken the chance to speak with Lazlo, who was asking her a question, and the man stepped forward, raising his voice once more.

"And what's the big idea, planting all these questions?" he continued. "That's your brother. Why does your brother get to ask you questions? Not really fair, is it? You're supposed to let the townsfolk come up with what they wanna know.

Not tell us what you want us to hear." He scoffed, looking around at those gathered, who hadn't realized what Wilda had been doing. "I think you should call on one of these folks here. Maybe Grant Klose over there. He's probably got a few burning questions."

"I don't, actually," Grant said, clearing his throat.

"Or—"

"Excuse *me*, young man!" Petula's voice rang out as she hurried over. Based on her expression, the man's name and address *hadn't* checked out on Max's rolls, which was all the more curious. If he wasn't a citizen of Pigsend, who was he? And why was he here?"

But those questions remained unanswered as the man spun on his heel and all but ran out of the crowd, disappearing into the night without another word.

Petula came up beside Bev, panting and trying to catch her breath. "Well, *he* certainly wasn't who he said he was."

"You checked the rolls that quickly?" Bev asked.

"Well, after Mr. Sterling and I went through the signatures, I wrote down every eligible voter in Pigsend alphabetically on my own list," she said. "I've got a pretty good memory, and I was sure I hadn't written that name, but I double-checked."

"Goodness," Bev said. "Where did he come

from, do you think?"

"Probably paid by one of the campaigns to cause trouble," Petula said, smoothing the front of her shirt. "I've seen it before in contentious campaigns. They send moles in to ask questions and catch the candidates flat-footed, to make themselves look better."

Bev turned back to the crowd. The man had focused on Wilda and Freddie, but not Hendry, who was examining her nails on the front step of the town hall and looking quite bored as everyone ignored her.

"Or it could very well be someone from out of town, interested in causing trouble," Petula said. "In any case, I'll ask around. As I said, we won't have any shenanigans during *this* election if I have anything to say about it."

She once again walked into the fray, and Bev lost sight of her in the crowd. But not a few moments later, Wilda and Freddie were being marched toward the town hall, and Hendry frowned as she stood.

"What's this about?" Hendry asked.

"The lot of you, *inside*," Petula said. "You, too, Bev. Since you were a witness."

Bev didn't think she should be included in this haranguing, but she didn't want to argue, so with a scowl, she followed the three candidates and Petula into the town hall. There was a dim candlelight illuminating the empty, cavernous space, though the sounds of the crowd outside echoed in. Although the candidates had been pulled from their posts, their surrogates were continuing in their place.

"What's this all about?" Freddie asked.

"I thought I was clear there were to be no shenanigans," Petula said. "That man who was heckling the two of you, he wasn't a citizen of Pigsend. I've got a hunch he was *hired* by one of you to disrupt the proceedings."

"Amateur hour, really," Hendry said, flipping a lock of hair over her shoulder. "If you're going to rabble rouse, you've got to hire someone from *inside* the town. Clearly, *someone* needs to read the rules and regulations book."

"*No one* should be hiring anyone to do anything," Petula said, glaring at Hendry.

The mayor shrugged. "I didn't say I did it. I've read the regulations, obviously. I'm conducting my campaign with the highest level of integrity."

"Is that why no one's showing up to your events?" Wilda asked.

Hendry growled.

"I didn't want to share this, but in light of tonight's event, I will: Pip Norris received a threatening letter, which is why he dropped out of the race." She cast a wary eye over the group. "Now, I want to know: which one of you sent it?"

Again, silence and confused looks. Though

Wilda looked a bit less confused than the rest, which piqued Bev's interest.

Petula didn't notice. "Very well. We have only two days until the election, and I *implore* each campaign to be on your best behavior. That includes both the candidate and their surrogates." She paused for effect. "*If* I find evidence of any sort of subterfuge or unfair play, that candidate will be immediately disqualified. Understand?"

Three nods.

"I also will allow any candidate, if that foul play is the result of their subordinates and not them personally, to bring that information forward anonymously and suffer no consequences." She cleared her throat. "You may bring this information to me or to Bev."

"Me?" Bev looked around.

"Yes, I've enlisted you to serve as an election monitor," Petula said with a half-smile. "Remember?"

"I've got the inn, and—"

"Please, Bev." Petula's gaze was sincere. "I know I can trust you."

She exhaled. "Fine."

"She was delivering cupcakes with Wilda earlier," Freddie started.

"As a favor to Lillie," Bev said. "I haven't officially said who I'm for yet. As every one of you has done something to make me against you."

Hendry scoffed. "Oh, come now, Bev, after all we've been through—"

Bev glared at her, and Hendry wisely clammed up.

"Then it's settled. Now, there's a large crowd outside hoping to hear from their candidates. If anyone sees any more troublemakers, find me or Bev, and we'll handle it. Understood?"

There was agreement across the board, and Petula simply nodded and marched toward the front door, Freddie and Hendry on her heels.

But Wilda, surprisingly, didn't move, waiting until the door closed before turning to her. "Do you have something to say, Wilda?"

"Yes." She cleared her throat. "I got a threatening letter, too."

Drop out of the race or I'll tell everyone you've got barus magic.

Chapter Thirteen

Bev stared at the note, shocked. "You…You've got barus magic?"

Wilda's face was bright red. "Well, not a lot of it. But enough to get on with."

"You're the one who gave Felicia the bauble to put in her pie, didn't you?" Bev said. "At the Harvest Festival. I thought she'd gotten that from the…well, there's another barus in the forest."

She nodded. "His name is Constantine. He's a full barus, whereas I'm only… Well, let's say I passed muster with Her Majesty's forces." She toyed with her hands as she avoided Bev's gaze. "My magic increases when I'm nearer to a source, as does every barus. When I go to the dark forest, I'm able to conjure all sorts of things." She twirled her fingers in the air. "Poof, whatever sort of magic I need."

"And how often have you needed magic?" Bev asked.

"A quiet spell here, a little pobyd magic there," she said. "But it's such a dangerous thing to do, I really only risk it around the Harvest Festival."

Bev pursed her lips. "So I remember."

"I don't think it's cheating if it's my magic," she said, redness creeping up her neck. "In any case, when poor Lillie was having her issues around the summer solstice, I was practically dripping with it, too. Had to make baubles to keep myself from levitating off the ground, you know..." She chuckled. "But it's all past now. Those baubles are buried in my root cellar for a rainy day. Nobody will ever find them."

Biscuit probably could. "You should think about getting rid of them. Unless..." Bev narrowed her gaze. "You aren't using them as bribes, are you?"

Her face screwed up in horror. "Bev! How dare you even insinuate such a thing?"

"Someone's sending blackmail letters," Bev said. "Clearly, all bets are off. And you'd asked Lillie to use her magic on the cupcakes—"

"Only so they wouldn't melt, Bev. Light magic, a touch of suggestion. Not a full-fledged barus bauble, capable of giving the person the kind of magic they need." She shook her head. "In any case,

I'm not willing to risk my neck for the mayor's job. At least, not risk it like *that*. Nobody knows about my barus powers."

"What about your cousin?" Bev asked. "The mayor? You were making barus baubles for her during the Harvest Festival, right?"

"Miranda?" Wilda fumbled with her fingers. "She knows about Constantine. In the forest. So I told her that the baubles came from him, and that I'd paid him handsomely."

"What about Lazlo? Does he know?"

A momentary pause, then she nodded. "He doesn't have the magic, though. Haven't a clue why it skipped him and came to me, but I've heard magic can be funny like that." She chewed her lip. "In any case, *no one* else is supposed to know. But here's this letter, and now..." She swallowed. "I'm so careful, Bev."

"When was the last time you went to the dark forest?" Bev asked.

"Ages ago. Before the Harvest Festival last year," she said. "Either someone's been sitting on this information until it was useful to them, or..." She tsked. "No one saw me make the baubles in my root cellar either. It was the dead of night, and everyone was running around trying to avoid getting eaten by a giant chicken."

Bev remembered all too well. She read the letter a few more times, hoping it would give her the answers she was looking for. The handwriting was identical to the other letters, which was something, at least. They were all coming from the same person. Someone who knew *everything* about everyone in town.

"So I got one, and Pip got one," Wilda said softly. "Which means it probably came from Freddie's campaign or from Hendry—"

"Hans got one," Bev said, looking up at her. After all, Wilda had gotten a letter, which presumably meant she was off the suspect list. "But he hasn't told Freddie. Wants him to stay in the race."

"Well, I'm not surprised," Wilda said. "They're quite intent on winning, those two. Nor am I surprised only *one* candidate didn't receive one."

Bev opened and closed her mouth. "Hendry hasn't told me she's received one, but it wouldn't surprise me if she did. If someone's threatening to reveal magical secrets, she's certainly got one to reveal."

"Yeah, and wouldn't it be like Hendry to pen a nasty letter to her competitors?" Wilda said, her campaigning tone coming back. "Thin out the herd, so to speak."

"That would be a bit hypocritical," Bev said.

"So? She'll do whatever it takes to win. You've seen her spell the entire town to get them to listen." Wilda crossed her arms. "We all know she's got mind-control powers. Maybe she's peeked into all our brains and heard our deepest, darkest secrets."

Bev wished she could tell Wilda that didn't make sense, that Hendry would never use her powers like that, but she couldn't. Hendry *had* used magic to get her way. Hendry *would* do whatever it took to win. And Hendry *was* trailing significantly in the polls. It was easy to win an election against no one.

And yet, it didn't fit with what Bev knew of Hendry. It was too obvious.

Wilda plastered on a smile. "Well, in any case, I'm obviously not dropping out, and, erm…I told *you* because you're our resident mystery solver, and you know Lillie's secret, so I assume you'll be careful with mine."

Bev nodded.

"But I'd appreciate it if you wouldn't tell Petula about any of it, *especially* the letter. I don't want to open a can of worms about what I've been threatened with, if you catch my meaning."

"Of course. And I'll ask that you keep my mention of Hans's letter secret, too."

Wilda nodded and turned toward the front doors. "Suppose I'd better get back out there before anyone suspects anything."

"You know," Bev said with a half-smile, "if Petula catches wind that you've been getting your supporters to ask questions, you might get in a little trouble. I don't think it's fair that only your campaign folks get to ask you questions."

Wilda's smile faded. "Erm, well. That's not... I don't..." She recovered. "Your point is well-taken, Bev. Well, off to meet my future constituents." She sauntered toward the door, as if she hadn't spilled her innermost secrets.

Bev waited a minute or two before walking toward the side door of the town hall. She wasn't keen on running into Petula again, as she didn't want to explain what she and Wilda had been talking about. Besides that, there was a sink full of dishes waiting for her, and she needed time to think.

Biscuit, ever the loyal friend, caught up with her halfway back to the inn. He walked beside her, wagging his tail, and Bev remembered when he'd first shown up, how he'd been able to scent Wilda's bauble from clear across town. How had he not scented the treasure trove in her root cellar?

Or had he, and he was on his best behavior now?

The inn was quiet, which was how Bev preferred it at this time of night, and she cleared the rest of the dishes from the front room, got a bucket of sudsy water from out back, and stood at the sink, scrubbing and thinking.

Pip, Freddie, and Wilda. All candidates, all received letters. All had magical secrets no one was supposed to know—some Bev hadn't even known, and she'd become something of a secret-keeper in town—but otherwise, there was very little connecting them. Pip shoed Freddie's horses, and Wilda made candles for the town, but they didn't run in the same social circles. And PJ, who was really the target of the first letter, certainly didn't spend loads of time with either person. In fact, the only thing Bev could say they had in common was they all revealed additional powers during the summer solstice.

What was Bev missing?

"We all know she's got mind-control powers. Maybe she's peeked into all our brains and heard our deepest, darkest secrets."

Bev really was loath to pin all this on Hendry, because it seemed so...sloppy. Hendry was very good at making people do what she wanted and making them think it was their idea. To send blackmail letters like this was absolutely out of character for her, even as badly as she wanted to win.

Besides that, would Hendry have known about PJ? Or even Wilda? She did have her finger on the pulse of the town, knew more about anyone than Bev would've guessed possible, but was that due to her place as mayor? Was it because she'd done her research or because she was using her abilities to pry?

Bev sighed, looking down at Biscuit, who sat

next to her.

"Suppose we should just ask her again, hm?" Bev said. "You should come with me, in case she tries to spell me."

Biscuit ruffed in agreement.

~

The next morning, Bev tended to her chores slowly, dreading the conversation with Hendry. She'd rehearsed what she was going to say and thought through every scenario that might come up, but still felt on the back foot, as she often did with Hendry. At least Biscuit's presence would embolden her. A simple nudge from the laelaps's nose would break any spell Hendry put on her—at least, Bev hoped that was still the case.

Before that, there was the morning to get through. Some of the farmers who'd come from farther away had rented a room at the inn for the night, so it was actually a full house. Bev finished her chores and sat at the front desk, watching the clock and waiting for the morning pastries.

Allen delivered them this morning, and the muffins were a cranberry-orange number that smelled divine. Almost too divine.

"I gave Lillie the morning off," he said. "Poor thing isn't getting any sleep with Wilda running campaign nonsense out of her house."

"I see." Bev questioned Lillie's logic of leaving him alone, but perhaps in her sleep-deprived state, she wasn't thinking. "So you made these?"

"Is there something wrong with them?" Allen asked.

"Erm, no." Bev picked one up and took a bite. Definitely laced with magic. "Perfect."

It's not the time.

And then, *Liar.*

Allen relaxed visibly as he bent down to pet Biscuit. Unsurprisingly, the laelaps was very interested in the muffins, too.

"What did Petula haul everyone into the town hall for?" Allen asked. "And who was that guy hassling Wilda?"

Bev had almost forgotten about the troublemaker. "I don't know. Petula thinks someone hired him to bother the candidates."

"He certainly did that," Allen said. "I've never seen Wilda so flustered. Who do you think—" He stopped, laughing. "Of course, it's probably Hendry. Didn't escape my notice that guy didn't bother *her*."

Perhaps because *nobody* was. "He's long gone, so I suppose that mystery will remain unsolved unless someone wants to come forward with the truth."

"You know," Allen leaned across the counter as if he had some juicy gossip, "Wilda's cousin got into town yesterday afternoon. Didn't really want to show herself at the question-and-answer, of course, but she was *very* surprised Petula was here."

"Really?" Bev frowned. "Because of the Harvest

Festival?"

"Apparently, Miranda did a bit of digging after last year. Petula used to be an election monitor, but there was some kind of scandal. She'd been accused of being bribed by one of the candidates, but it wasn't ever proven. So she basically got demoted to investigating Harvest Festivals. And the soldiers that came with her were there to watch *her*, not the festival."

Bev's brows rose, and she glanced at the staircase. "That's certainly a revelation. She told me this is her first election back in her old job. That's why she's so keen on making sure everything's on the up-and-up." Bev paused. "They never found her guilty, then?"

"You'll have to ask Miranda," Allen said as a door upstairs opened and closed. "But it might be worth looking at Petula to see if *she* might be the source of these letters—or someone out to get her."

The woman herself appeared at the top of the stairs, and Allen took that as a sign to leave. Bev tried to keep her face neutral as Petula descended to the front room, but the information Allen had given her had been surprising, to say the least.

"Morning, Bev," Petula said. "I do hope you aren't too cross with me volunteering you officially as an election monitor."

"You aren't the first person to volunteer me for something," Bev said. "Seems to be routine around here."

"Well, as I said, it's hard to find someone who is truly neutral in a town like this. And you're that person." She picked up a muffin and took a bite. "Oh, these are *extra* heavenly this morning, aren't they? My compliments to the baker."

"I'm sure you miss getting to taste all the festival goods," Bev said, dancing around the question she really wanted to ask. "Do you miss judging them?"

"Oh, a little, for sure. But election monitoring is my real passion." She finished her muffin and glanced at the basket. "May I have another?"

Bev picked up the basket and offered it to her, and she gladly took another.

"Did Ms. Murtagh have anything to say last night? I noticed she didn't follow us out into the town square immediately."

"Just wanted to thank me for my help. The bakers were swamped with work, and she needed help getting cupcakes to the farmers farther out of town, so I volunteered," Bev said. "Though I can't say it was really helpful. The cupcakes were intercepted by Freddie before they got into the hands of voters."

Petula frowned. "Do tell."

Bev gave her the details, and Petula's scowl deepened. "That's certainly skirting the line of the rules. Delivering cupcakes to undecided voters could be seen as a bribe, and speaking to a crowd could be considered a campaign event, which requires my presence and approval." She sighed. "It really is a tough job to have one election monitor for an election this size."

Allen's comments settled in Bev's mind. "Shouldn't you write to your superiors to send someone to help?"

"Oh, no time for that." She adjusted her pin. "I have to say, though, it will be quite the report I'll deliver. They'll be pleased to see how much effort went into making this a fair election."

And will that result in a promotion? "Are you going to include the letters?"

Petula sighed. "Sadly, yes. I must include every detail, even the unsavory ones. I've already written my assessment of Mr. Norris, and if any more letters should pop up, I'll have to include those as well." She pursed her lips. "If only we'd been able to catch that perfidious troublemaker last night. I'm dying to know who paid him to be there."

"You're sure someone did?" Bev asked.

She nodded. "There's no other reason someone from out of town would travel all the way to Pigsend. No, someone is keen on tilting the scales to one candidate, and I'm going to find out who it is." She beamed at Bev. "Would you mind accompanying me to Mayor Hendry's office this morning?"

Bev nearly slipped off her stool. "Hendry? You

suspect her?"

"I have several things I need to chat with her about, then I've got to spend the day between Freddie and Wilda's. The debate is tonight, and I understand there's going to be another party at each house beforehand." She cleared her throat. "So, if you're willing to go now…it would be quite helpful. I find that…speaking with Hendry with someone else present tends to…well, I don't want to say that there's anything *amiss* with Mayor Hendry, but—"

"Say no more," Bev said, waving her off. "Happy to come with you." She nodded to Biscuit, who was at her heels. "And Biscuit will come, too."

Chapter Fourteen

If Petula thought it strange that Biscuit was coming along, she didn't say anything. She was almost *nervous* about speaking with Hendry, which was very odd indeed. Petula had always been the sort who knew she was in charge and expected everyone to fall in line. To see her fidgeting so was concerning.

"Is everything all right?" Bev asked.

"Oh, perfectly!" Petula's smile was so bright it was almost blinding. "Just lots to do today. Wouldn't it have been lovely if Mr. Silver's house wasn't so far?"

"And what are you doing down there?"

"He's requested my presence for a small

gathering for the farmers who haven't been able to make any other events."

"I thought all the campaign events had to be attended by all the candidates?" Bev asked.

"Well, not exactly," Petula said. "A candidate is able to host their own event, like they did on the first night. In this case, Mr. Silver made a compelling case, so he's allowed to host a second one. I gave permission as long as he invited them to the candidate debate later today, and, of course, I was there."

Bev nodded. "Is anyone else doing something similar today?"

"Goodness, I hope not." She put her hand over her head. "I do prefer elections to occur later in the season, when it's not quite so hot. But when Hendry wrote to us a few weeks ago, an exception made sense."

"What was her reasoning?" Bev asked.

"Well, that there was one candidate, the last election was sparsely attended, and the upcoming Harvest Festival might—" Petula stopped and closed her mouth.

"Might what?" Bev asked.

"Oh, you'll find out if it happens," she said, evasively. "But it's not my position to say at this point in time."

Bev couldn't imagine what sort of secret Petula had about the Harvest Festival, but that thought was set aside as she opened the front doors of the town hall and heard raised voices echoing from Hendry's office. She and Petula shared a glance before rushing toward it.

There, they found Hendry arguing with Miranda, who was the less aggrieved of the two.

"I mean, if you can't run your own election—" she said, twirling her hand in the air and shrugging.

"Good, Petula is here," Hendry cut her off with a glare. "Ms. Banks, you might want to know that there's an external election interferer in town."

"I'm not interfering in *anything*," Miranda said. "I'm simply here to advise and guide my cousin in her campaign. No more, no less." She paused. "I was merely *saying* that it's not my fault Mayor Hendry's political campaign is so dead it's practically six feet under already."

Hendry scowled. "The election isn't over until it's *over*. Plenty of time for me to make up lost ground."

"If you even finish second, I'll resign my post," Miranda said before turning to Petula and Bev. She eyed Petula with the sort of arrogance Bev had seen during the festival. "Ms. Banks, it's lovely to see you again."

"And you, Mayor Twinsly." Petula's smile was polite, and showed no hint that she was aware Miranda knew about her job misfortunes and was telling people all over town. "So good of you to come help your family. Your election isn't until next year, correct?"

"Yes, we've got a different cycle in Middleburg, as our elections are held in the spring." She sighed, as if Pigsend were a quaint little thing to be pitied. "It is quite the job to be mayor of such a large city, but when my cousin wrote to me, I had to take a day or two off. I've got a sizable staff," she looked around the empty town hall as if proving a point, "and they're so good at their jobs, it's easy for me to step away for a bit."

"So what you're saying is that your staff runs the town?" Hendry asked, earning a glare from Miranda. "And Middleburg isn't *that* much bigger than Pigsend. Three hundred people, *maybe*, live in the city limits."

"We count five hundred and seventy-two on our election rolls," she said, nodding to Petula, as if the other woman would confirm it. When Petula didn't, Miranda sniffed loudly. "In any case, I suppose I'll see you next year to monitor our election? Are you in charge of this whole region or...?"

"Not *in charge*, no," Petula said, looking a little uncomfortable.

"No? But a woman of your stature..." Miranda let out a small laugh. "Oh, that's right. There was that little *misunderstanding* from Modon."

Petula's cheeks went pink, and for the first time since Bev had known her, the election monitor was thrown off her footing. "Ah, you heard about that?"

"Everyone's heard about that," Miranda drawled, looking at Hendry. The Pigsend mayor wasn't surprised by the information, but even if she was, Bev doubted she'd give Miranda the satisfaction.

"Erm, I haven't," Bev said. Though she'd heard a bit from Allen, it would be good to hear it straight from the horse's mouth. "What misunderstanding?"

"Just a little kerfuffle. Nothing really to talk about," Petula said. "Someone thought that I might have been doing something wrong. I wasn't—"

"It was a *bribe*, wasn't it?" Miranda pressed. "Goodness, who would've thought such a thing of Ms. Petula Banks? I can only assume it was a baseless accusation with no evidence—"

"They, erm, well, they had a few things they thought could've..." Petula's face was turning redder by the moment. "Unfortunately, in my younger days, I wasn't quite as invested in the rules and didn't understand the differences between this and that, you know." She adjusted the rule book in her hand as if it were her lifeline. "It was all cleared up, though."

"*Was* it cleared up?" Miranda said, leaning in closer. "Because as I understand it, for an election with multiple candidates, you should have two assistants with you."

"There *was* only supposed to be one candidate,

but several others joined the race—"

"Do your superiors know that?" Miranda pressed.

Once again, Petula was caught looking like her clothes were suddenly itchy. "Not quite yet. Things are moving so fast. I plan to write it all up in my report, you know. Leave nothing out. These things do happen. Surprises. Especially out in the country." She glanced at her timepiece. "Goodness, look at that. I've got to be getting down to Mr. Silver's for his campaign speech—um, barbecue." She was now so flustered, even her hair looked frazzled. "Bev, can you take over here?"

Bev frowned. "But I don't—"

She was gone before Bev could finish her statement.

"Honestly, Miranda, could you be more abrasive?" Hendry drawled. "Can't say it's the smartest strategy to bully the election monitor."

"I'm trying to get to the truth," Miranda said, putting her hand to her heart. "I owe it to my cousin to make sure her election is conducted as fairly and impartially as possible. And if it is without the proper precautions—"

"Oh, stuff it," Hendry snapped. "You liked seeing her uncomfortable. Never forgave her for ruining your big plans to move the Harvest Festival."

Bev would've thought such a thing beneath the

Middleburg mayor, but a flash of color lit her face. "We've got plans. Petitions to the regional governor. A spring festival would be quite lovely, you know?"

"Yes, be sure to show off the unripe fruit," Hendry said with a mean smile. "We can all celebrate by getting sick."

Miranda glowered and turned her attention on Bev. "Weren't you here for something, innkeeper? Or are you adding lurking like a ghost to your repertoire?"

Bev didn't actually know what Petula wanted to talk with Hendry about, but Bev did have a few things to ask the mayor herself. "I need to speak with Hendry alone, if that's all right?"

"Mm. Are you sure you want to do that?" Miranda said. "You might end up with an addled brain, or clucking like a chicken, or—"

"That's quite enough, Miranda," Hendry said. "Bev, please have a seat. Happy to answer *any* question you might have. Goodness knows, I answered so many last night. But I couldn't help noticing you disappeared after Petula's little speech. And Wilda, too, hung around. Care to share what that was about?"

Bev glanced at Miranda, who didn't know Wilda had spoken with Bev. "She wanted to chat about Lillie, her roommate. Her birthday's coming up. Wanted to do something nice for her."

Based on their expressions, neither Hendry nor

Miranda bought that. "I see," Miranda said.

"In any case, I do have to get back to the inn, so if you don't mind giving us a bit of privacy," Bev said to Miranda as she sat in front of Hendry.

Miranda wavered in the doorway for a moment longer then swept from the town hall, taking the rain cloud of attitude with her.

"I thought she'd *never* leave," Hendry said, sinking down into her chair. But before she relaxed, she finally noticed Biscuit standing at the ready next to Bev's feet. "Why is your dog here?"

"Because I have some questions to ask you, and I want to make sure they get answered without you sending me on my merry way," Bev said. "Now—"

"I have no idea who sent that letter to Pip," Hendry said. "As I told you."

Bev held her breath, waiting for Hendry to admit she'd received one, too. When she just looked at Bev expectantly, Bev exhaled. "So you haven't gotten one?"

"Why would *I* get a letter like that?" Hendry scoffed. "Who in their right mind would want to blackmail *me*? Everyone in town knows better." Bev fiddled with her hands so much that Hendry noticed her discomfort. "Wait...don't tell me someone else got one."

"A few someone elses," Bev said.

Hendry sat back, looking honestly surprised. "So what...because I didn't, I'm a suspect?"

"Actually, no," Bev said. "It's too obvious. You're far too clever to do something like that."

Hendry actually smiled, a pretty smile and the most genuine one Bev had ever seen on her. "Thank you, Bev. That really means a lot."

"But if you are the one sending letters, do me a favor and tell me," Bev said. "Because there's nothing I hate more than running about town trying to investigate something when the culprit's sitting around watching me waste my time on dead ends."

"I swear, on your beloved inn and the grave of Wim McKee, that I did not write those letters," Hendry said. "I wouldn't even know what would cause Pip to drop out of the race. Did he shoe a horse wrong?" She chuckled. "I mean, I could see someone holding a grudge, but—"

"This isn't funny," Bev said. "And I need to know if you know anything."

"I don't, and that's the truth," she said.

"Then why did you know to go to Pip's event after yours was a bust?" Bev asked. "How did you know he was going to drop out?"

She took a breath. "You asked me if I'd written him a threatening letter, remember? After that, I saw him mucking about town looking like he was about to cry. I figured it probably wasn't a stretch that he'd lost his nerve."

Bev relaxed, only a little. "I see."

"Besides that, I knew he wasn't actually serious. You know how it goes, sometimes. You get a wild hair then realize it's far too much work, and you're in over your head. Especially with hiring Earl as his campaign manager?" She scoffed. "Now Wilda? Freddie? Those are real competitors. They've got their stuff together." She shifted. "Also, we had a *lot* of food. His house was closer than Freddie's, and I wouldn't be caught dead bringing *anything* to Wilda's." She gestured to the empty door. "Going to take all day to air out the stink of her cousin's perfume."

Bev could barely smell a thing. "And what about not telling Petula about the other candidates? Rustin told me you'd been gathering information on Wilda and Freddie in preparation for the campaign."

"I gather information on *everyone*," Hendry said. "But I didn't know anyone was actually serious about running. These things are usually a sleepy affair. Half the town doesn't vote, either, so…"

"So you hoped with a low turnout, you'd eke out a victory?" Bev asked. "Then Freddie, Wilda, and Pip stood up, and your plans were ruined."

"Honestly, Bev…" Hendry sat back and chewed her perfectly red lip. "You might want to turn your focus onto Petula. As much as I hate to admit that Miranda's right, there was a *lot* of scuttlebutt about her abysmal demotion from election monitor to Harvest Festival judge. Maybe *she's* sending the letters so Wilda and Freddie will drop out, thus keeping her from having to report to her superiors that she oversaw an election with multiple candidates by herself."

"That's preposterous," Bev said.

"Is it? Someone might go to great lengths to keep their recently reacquired job." Hendry gestured to her office. "I'm moving heaven and earth to keep the one I've had for years."

Bev chewed her lip. "But how would she even know the details these letters claim to know? *I* didn't even know half of them."

"Maybe she's got a secret journal like that Claude fellow. Remember, he was making a list of suspected magicals in town when he was mucking up our Harvest Festival."

Bev nodded.

"Maybe Petula took a page out of his book. Or read his book, you never know. They were in town at the same time." She picked up a piece of paper stamped with the queen's seal. "She's staying at *your* inn. Might be worthwhile to snoop around."

"I don't snoop—"

"Bev, love, I'm *quite* busy with this job I have until I no longer have it, so if that'll be all…"

~

As a rule, Bev didn't venture into her guests' rooms when they were rented. She had, of course, in dire circumstances, but her suspicions about Petula didn't rise to that level. If anything, Hendry could be sending her on a wild goose chase. But Hendry had planted the seed in Bev's mind, as had Miranda, and Bev had done this enough times not to leave any stone unturned.

Petula was, unsurprisingly, not at the inn, but Bev didn't go upstairs immediately. She tidied the front room, though it was already tidy. She checked on her bread dough, which was fine. It wasn't quite time to start dinner, either, though she could speak with the butchers. Still, she couldn't bring herself to leave the inn, not when she had so many unanswered questions.

"What do you reckon, Biscuit?" she asked.

The laelaps unfurled his tongue in a smile.

"That's not very helpful." She adjusted her apron. "Maybe a quick look around. In the interest of being helpful. Maybe there's something to wash, you know?"

She continued rationalizing as she grabbed her master key, ascended the stairs, found Petula's room, and put the key in the door. She hesitated before opening it, giving herself one final chance to come to her senses. But Biscuit pawed at the door crack, and it swung open.

Petula's room was neat and tidy, a perfect microcosm of the woman herself. There were several neat tunics folded and ready in the dresser. Her satchel was empty and stashed away. The bed, even, was made—almost as nicely as Bev made it for her guests. There was nothing, really, of note.

Except that, in and of itself, was somewhat surprising. Petula had said she'd been keeping copious notes and was already halfway through writing her report for her superiors. So where was that report? She could've taken it with her, but the only thing Petula had been carrying earlier was her rules and regulations book. Plus, shouldn't there be some kind of evidence? A journal, a notepad, something?"

"Maybe it's stashed in there?" Bev muttered, walking to the dresser and opening the other drawers. Empty.

"What are you doing in here?"

Bev spun around to find Petula on the threshold of her room.

Chapter Fifteen

"I was looking for...erm...the report," Bev said, scrambling for an excuse. "The one you're sending to your superiors. Wanted to see if there was anything I might've missed. So much is happening around town, some important detail might've gotten lost in the shuffle."

Petula eyed her suspiciously. "I haven't exactly... written it yet."

"You haven't?" Bev furrowed her brow. "But you told Miranda..."

"Anything to keep her from running her mouth," Petula huffed, walking in and shutting the door behind her. "She's so...well, she's not my favorite person. And I believe she has it out for me after I ruined her plans to move the Harvest Festival last year. That's the only reason she went digging in my past."

"I can't imagine she'd thought she'd see you again," Bev said. "Or that she was that upset about the Harvest Festival."

"Believe you me, she *was*," Petula said, crossing the room to adjust a tunic Bev had touched. "I saw her in Queen's Capital, eagerly speaking with my superiors. Good thing I know how to cover myself. They were wise to her games and sent her on her way without a second word. She's still trying to lobby for a spring festival, but she's dreaming."

Bev watched her carefully for a moment then asked, "You aren't trying to scare everyone but Hendry out of the race so you won't get in trouble?"

Petula's eyes widened, and she covered her heart. "Bev, do you really think I'd do such a thing? First of all, I don't know half the people in this town, and I definitely don't know their secrets."

"Maybe you have Claude's notebook," Bev prompted.

"Claude." She snorted. "You best believe I wrote a sternly worded letter to *his* commanding officer. Masquerading as a judge. We both work for the queen. The least he could've done was tell me what he was. Not as if I would've shared his secret." She shook herself, as if she were still offended by the entire episode. "Outrageous."

"You didn't answer my question," Bev said.

"No, Bev. I'm not writing the letters. Nor do I have Claude's notebook. In fact, I didn't even get a peek at it, other than when I was with you in the town hall. After all, he left right after he was revealed to be a fake, and he took his evidence with him." She crossed her arms. "And I haven't a clue who might have it out for Pip Norris, or what they could've sent him that was so terrifying that he dropped out. So you're looking at the wrong person."

Bev watched her for a moment then glanced at Biscuit, who let out a small ruff in acceptance. "Very well."

"Really, Bev. How you could've thought—"

"You do have a bit of a motive," Bev said. "Wanting to keep this election to one candidate so you don't get in trouble with your superiors. After all, you told them Hendry was the only one running, right? And if there was more than one candidate, you should've had help, right?"

She let out a laugh. "If anything, they'll be pleased with how I've handled it. This isn't the first contentious election, nor the first where more candidates than anticipated joined. It's quite common, I assure you. The usual course of action is to find a helper or two in the general population." She gestured to Bev. "Which I've done. I can show you the section in the rules and regulations document that explains the protocols, if you're so interested."

Bev perhaps should've considered that instead of believing Hendry and Miranda. "I'm sorry for snooping. Miranda put the idea in my mind that you might be responsible, what with your...erm..."

"My history?" She shook her head. "Well, it's not very nice but not nearly as sordid as Miranda would have you believe. If anything, there was a concerted effort to tarnish my reputation precisely *because* it's so sterling." She sat on the bed. "Modon was run by a group of individuals very used to getting their way. It was right after the war ended, and the town was on the king's side. They weren't too keen on my presence, and when I didn't—*ahem*—want to do things the way they'd always done it, they *really* weren't happy. But I had a contingent of soldiers with me, so there was nothing they could do outright." She paused. "So, one of them had the brilliant idea of trapping me in a compromising position. I was told the city was hosting a party in my honor. Seemed innocuous enough, and I was naive enough to think I could trust the local mayor. Hours after I arrived, I realized that while it *was* in my honor, it was paid for by the mayor out of their campaign funds—a clear violation of the rules. And enough of a question that my superiors took action."

"I'm so sorry to hear that," Bev said. "And you

were demoted to Harvest Festivals?"

"A mutual decision, to be honest. I was a bit *unnerved* by the whole thing. I thought Harvest Festivals and one-candidate elections would be a little safer, you know?" She shivered. "I didn't realize that those awful people in Modon had spread false rumors about me until quite recently. Not that I care what people think..." Based on her expression, she clearly did. "In any case, that's the truth of my *sordid* past."

Bev certainly felt for her. "That means I'm back to square one."

"Surely, you have some theories?"

"Several," Bev said. "But the truth is, none of them will make a lick of sense until I find out how people have figured out all these...well, secrets."

"Secrets? Plural?" She sat up. "Has someone else received a letter?"

Bev nodded. "If it's all the same to you, I'm not going to tell you which candidates. The fewer people who know—"

"The smaller the suspect list, yes, I understand." She pursed her lips. "Well, it doesn't seem to have worked, as no more candidates have dropped out."

"This is bigger than the election," Bev said. "I have to figure this out before things escalate."

"The debate is tonight," Petula said. "There will be anonymous questions from the audience. What if you wrote one asking them about the threats? Catch them off guard, so to speak."

"They won't answer, not outright like that," Bev said.

"I hear you're the resident mystery solver in town," Petula said. "I have faith you'll figure something out. You have..." She checked her timepiece. "Five hours."

~

Bev was starting to really chafe under this expectation that she'd solve everyone's problems, especially when she had an inn to run. But as she worked on dinner, she mulled over her options and tried to figure out what in the world she could ask that would "put them on the spot," as Petula had said. Obviously asking, "Are you behind the anonymous threats?" wasn't going to work. Nor was the very blunt question of, "Do you know any secrets about your fellow candidates?" But that was all she could think of, and the pressure was starting to get to her as the minutes ticked down.

For the millionth time, she dove back into her memories of PJ's almost-transformation. Earl's workshop had gone up in flames, then Alice's barn, then the seamstress shop with Vicky inside. Certainly possible that someone had seen the kids out and about, but if they had, they'd have spoken up during the town meeting discussing the events.

The town meeting.

Bev lifted her knife from the potato, an idea

springing to mind. During the meeting about the destroyed buildings, Bev had handed out lavender scones covered in icing—and baked with a *touch* of magic. It was Hendry's idea; she'd thought exposing the culprit to a bit of magic would trigger a small reaction, thus revealing them.

Of course, it had triggered a not-small reaction, as PJ had burned down the schoolhouse unbeknownst to anyone but Grant and Valta.

But to slip something like that into a baked good…would such a thing work twice? And instead of a hint of magic, would it be possible to create something with a truth-telling component to it? One that would prompt the candidates to answer if asked the very blunt, very obvious questions?

It was, unfortunately, the only solution Bev could come up with. But to get that kind of magic, she'd have to go next door.

"Hm…" Lillie rubbed her chin. "I mean, it's *possible*, I think? I've never done anything like that before. Usually, I'm making confections to taste good, not to make anyone do anything." She paused. "But you really want to serve them tonight during the debate? That hardly seems fair, does it?"

"Well, I'd hope the candidates would be honest," Bev said.

"You would think, but…" Lillie sighed. "Wilda's been practicing *not* telling the whole truth with Miranda. She's got all her lines rehearsed to dance around the questions. Forcing her to tell the truth up there on stage..."

Bev snapped her fingers as she had an idea. "You put a time limit on those cupcakes, right?"

She nodded.

"Maybe this suggestion could last five minutes after the person ate it?" Bev said. "I could serve them before the debate then ask whatever questions I needed."

"That...could work." Lillie nodded slowly. "I don't think it could compel them to tell you something they *really* didn't want to share. But it would loosen their tongues a bit. It may get you closer to the culprit."

"I'll take it," Bev said.

"Just one problem," Lillie said with an affable smile. "There's no way Hendry or Freddie will eat something I bake."

"I can make it," Bev said. "Maybe you could infuse magic in the sugar?"

"Brilliant," Lillie said with a smile. "You do know what you're doing, don't you, Bev?"

"And perhaps give me a suggestion of what to bake," Bev said. "I've already done magical scones, so I don't think that'll work twice."

Lillie tapped her chin. "Something pretty simple, I'd think. You don't have a lot of time to make something complex like a turnover." Her face lit up. "What about a sweet bread? We've got a new crate of lemons in the back. I can give you a couple. A lemon blueberry bread with a sweet icing would be delicious. I'm sure I've got a recipe around here somewhere." She walked to the shelves, where Fernley's recipe cards were stored in a neat box. She plucked one out of the cards and handed it to Bev. "Here you go. Help yourself to the blueberries in the root cellar, too. And if I were you, I'd use lemon juice in the icing as well, though the recipe doesn't call for that."

"Thank you." Bev inspected the card for a moment. "Do you think this will work?"

"It's worth a shot," Lillie said. "Give me a few minutes to work on the sugar."

~

Bev grabbed a small crate of blueberries and a few lemons, and Lillie brought over the sugar that she'd infused with magic. As the pobyd walked in the door, she was a bit starry-eyed, and when Bev asked what was wrong, she started talking.

"I really am considering moving to Silverkeep, but I don't want to leave Allen in the lurch. I also can't stop thinking about what I did in Lower Pigsend, and sometimes I'm embarrassed to even look in the mirror. And—" She clamped her hand over her mouth. "Goodness. Sorry. I had to *really* be intentional with the sugar, and..." She cleared her throat. "I should go hide in my room before I tell anyone else anything."

Bev smiled. "Thank you for this."

"I rather hope it's Wilda, because I'm so tired of our house being used as a campaign headquarters all hours of the night, and I don't like her cousin…" Lillie took a breath. "Dearie me. Yes. Need to hide."

She scampered out of the kitchen, and Bev laughed. The sugar sat in its canister, almost ominously, and Bev was a little nervous to touch it. As she measured and mixed her ingredients, she used a spoon to add the magic-infused sugar and mixed it together with that instead of by hand.

The blueberries—still plump from the solstice shenanigans—were folded in with the rest of the ingredients, and she squeezed the juice from one of the lemons after adding the zest as well. Then she poured the bread mixture into one of her trusty bread tins and placed it in her oven.

Biscuit had wandered in by now and was sniffing the sugar canister while his tail wagged feverishly. Bev chuckled and patted him on the head as his tongue darted along the floor searching for a little that had fallen off the table.

"Perhaps a good thing you can't talk," Bev said. "You'd be spilling all my secrets to everyone, you know?"

The bread came out an hour later, smelling heavenly. The blueberries had burst, threading the bread crumb with blue veins that steamed and bubbled. While it cooled, Bev made the icing, melting the magic-laced sugar and lemon juice together on the stove and slowly adding milk to it to create a thin icing. When the bread had cooled, she drizzled the icing on top and set the whole thing on the corner of the kitchen table while she tackled the rest of dinner.

"Suppose it'll work," Bev said to Biscuit, as she took the meat out of the oven and carved it. "Just have to make sure just the candidates eat it."

That was going to be the rub. Hendry *was* quite clever and would know something was up. Bev didn't make bread like this, and it had been Hendry's idea to add magic to the scones earlier in the year. Wilda and Freddie might also be suspicious, though Freddie was less likely to jump to conclusions than Wilda. Petula might have questions, too.

"Maybe if I make it a competition between them," Bev said with a chuckle. "The only one who doesn't eat it will be guilty."

Biscuit let out a small ruff.

"Well, I'm sure I'll come up with something."

Dinner was well-attended, with lots of not-quite-out-of-towners coming in to hear the debate between the candidates. Bev, who'd had to pay for her own meat this evening, was happy she'd ordered more than she'd anticipated, as there was very little left once everyone had been served. Bev took pity on Biscuit, who was watching the food dwindle with a sad expression, and tossed him a big piece.

"That, and you had a ton of potato skins," Bev said to his depressed face. "Fear not, Biscuit. The election is over tomorrow night. Then you'll have all the dinner you can stand."

"Did I see something iced and delicious in there?" Bardoff asked, walking up to Bev with his empty plate. "Did the bakers make it?"

"I did, actually." Bev cleared her throat. "For the event tonight. For the candidates."

"Those politicians don't need you to make them anything," Etheldra grumbled. "Already taking up enough of our time as it is. You should give it to us, instead. We'd appreciate it more."

Bev didn't want to *think* about a world where Etheldra was even more truthful. "I'll make another for you tomorrow, Etheldra. Or I'll ask the bakers to. It's Fernley's recipe."

"Mm." The tea shop owner eyed her. "And why are *you* baking it? Up to something, Bev?"

"No more than usual," Bev said.

"Say no more." Etheldra tapped her nose. "Bardoff, Earl," she barked to the two behind her, "let's go. Gotta get a front row seat to tonight's debate. I have a feeling it's going to be *very interesting*."

Chapter Sixteen

As she had the previous nights, Bev followed the gaggle of diners from the inn to the town hall, where the debate was to take place. Petula hadn't returned from Freddie's campaign event for dinner, so Bev had set aside a plate for her to eat later. She wasn't sure if Freddie had food, but after hearing Petula's story about the attempted bribery, she probably wouldn't eat anything offered by a candidate.

She presliced the blueberry bread and carried only the slices with her, hoping she could avoid having to share with anyone else. Besides the candidates, Bev was hoping to give Gore and Miranda a slice of bread, especially the latter. She had a feeling the Middleburg mayor had more secrets than anyone.

The town hall was already bustling when they arrived, with a queue of people lined up in front of a table filled with cards and quills. A sign indicated people should write their questions on a card and leave them in the nearby crate, which was already filled with them.

Bev scanned the room, finding Wilda and Miranda standing near the front, deep in conversation. Since she didn't see any other candidate there, she headed in their direction, hoping she could convince them to eat her bread without raising too much suspicion.

"What's that?" Wilda asked as Bev approached.

"Erm, a little pick-me-up before the show begins," Bev said. "Thought it would be a nice treat."

"Did Lillie make it?" Miranda asked. "Or Allen?"

"No, I did. Thought it would be fairer that way," Bev said. "Try it."

Neither one looked at the bread.

"Erm. It's Fernley's recipe," Bev said. "Lillie gave it to me, but don't mention it to anyone else."

The mention of Lillie seemed to tip the scale in her favor, and they both took a piece. "Oh, this is quite good. Did the lemons come from here, too?" Wilda asked.

"Yes, some leftovers from the cupcakes," Bev said. She didn't know how long it would take to kick in, but time was of the essence. "Looks to be a nice crowd, eh?"

"Small, pathetic little town," Miranda said. "You know, when we have elections they're three times the size. We've got a town hall that's—"

"Yes, *Miranda*, I know your town's bigger than mine," Wilda drawled. "You've only mentioned it a hundred times since you've been here."

"And you're being awfully catty for someone I've traveled a long way to help. Your campaign was absolutely in the ditch when I arrived, and thanks to me, it's been revived."

"Really?" Bev leaned in. "What've you done, Miranda?"

"Well, very clearly had the idea to walk the countryside, as Hendry had already done. Take cupcakes to them, too. Of course, you messed that up by letting your opponent eat them, so I can't help you there." Miranda continued rattling off the various things she'd helped with, including prepping Wilda for the debate. "And here you are, ungrateful as ever."

"I'm not ungrateful. I don't like hearing you besmirch my town," Wilda said. "Especially after all the time and effort *I've* put in. There were things happening here before I even called you in."

"Like what?" Bev asked, glancing at the clock.

Lillie had said the spell was good for five minutes, and that time was rapidly coming to a close.

"Making friends in town. Finding out what people disliked Hendry for. Repairing my reputation after the disastrous Harvest Festival," Wilda said. "Absolutely gutted that was pinned on me, you know."

"Well, don't worry, because assuming you win this election, there won't be a Pigsend Harvest Festival to speak of," Miranda said before closing her mouth and clearing her throat. "Erm. I mean, the people will have forgotten about last year's problems."

Bev eyed her suspiciously, but Miranda eyed her right back.

"What was in that bread?" Miranda asked.

"Just lemon and blueberry," Bev said with a half-smile. "Oh, there's Hendry. Got to take her a slice, too. And if you see Freddie, send him my way, will you?"

Bev dashed away, hoping she hadn't aroused too much suspicion. Clearly, the spell worked a little better than expected—and quickly, too. She'd think about what Miranda said about the Harvest Festival later, as the time for the debate was drawing closer.

Hendry was working the room to little interest and scowled when Bev walked up.

"What do you want?" Hendry asked as Bev approached with a smile. "And what is that?"

"Thought you and the candidates could use a little treat," Bev said. "I was hoping it would help with everyone's mood, you know?"

"Mm." Hendry pursed her lips. "The last time you baked something for everyone, it was laced with magic. I can only assume this is the same."

"That's not fair," Bev said. "I made a crumble a few weeks ago. That didn't have any magic in it."

She snorted. "Yes, as I recall, it was the antidote for magic." She eyed Bev suspiciously. "But you aren't the baking-sweets type, as you once told me. Why would you go to the trouble of making such a thing? And for the candidates? You aren't *that* nice, Bev."

"I am, too," Bev said. "And since Lillie and Allen are on Wilda's team, I didn't think the rest of you'd trust them to make anything." She paused. "Wilda *and* Miranda both ate a slice, if you're worried about it."

Hendry considered her then, to Bev's delight, took the offered slice. "Suppose if it's good for the goose, it's good for the gander."

"Yes, can't possibly let Miranda get away with anything, you know," Bev said, sensing she might've found her angle. "After all, what if that extra bit of sugar gives her the edge?"

Hendry scowled, and Bev got the distinct impression Hendry could see right through her. But the mayor took a small bite, sniffed as if she were expecting something else, then swallowed.

"Just be sure to offer one to Freddie, too," Hendry said. "Because it wouldn't be fair to him, you know. The only one who didn't get a piece. One might think you're *up to something*, Bev."

"I'm not up to anything," Bev said. "I'm trying to get to the truth about who's sending the letters."

"It's not me," Hendry said, holding her chin high. "But we've already discussed that at length. Surely, you asked Wilda and Miranda while they were under the influence of your funny bread. I'm sure they had loads to tell you about the nonsense they've gotten into. Freddie, too. And I don't trust Gore. He's a little too invested in this campaign, if you ask me."

"What else do you think?" Bev said.

"I think you put something in that bread to get me to reveal secrets," Hendry said. "And I think I don't have any to reveal, and I'm a bit offended you still suspect me. If anything, I'm being framed."

"Who would want to frame you?" Bev asked. She didn't want to add *because your campaign is already failing*, because that might not be taken too well.

"The very same people I mentioned." Hendry nodded to the front door. "Including the opponent who just showed up. Why's Petula with him, anyway? Is she picking sides?"

Freddie had arrived with his usual group of

farmers, along with Petula. The monitor was looking quite tired and sunburned, as if she'd spent the entire day out in the fields with the farmers. Bev squared her shoulders and walked over, intending on sharing a slice with Freddie and Gore.

"Evening, all. I come bearing a treat for the candidate," Bev said.

"I'm not into sweets," Freddie said, not even looking at her.

"Wilda had a slice," Bev said. "And Hendry, too. You don't want them to have an unfair advantage, do you?"

"I'd say we've got the advantage now, as they're going to be sluggish from all the sugar," Gore said, holding a slew of cards he was priming Freddie with.

Bev glanced at Petula, and the election monitor peered at the bread greedily. "Oh, what will a little sweet do?" Petula asked. "I think it's perfectly lovely. Thank you, Bev, for the thought. I know I'm particularly famished."

And before Bev could stop her, Petula picked up one of the two remaining slices and ate it.

"Delicious."

"C'mon, Fred." Hans nudged his husband. "You haven't eaten anything all day, either. You'll need a bit of something so you've got all your wits about you. I'm sure somebody's got something up their sleeve, you know? Can't trust that Wilda—or Hendry, for that matter. But you can trust Bev.

She's…well, she's Bev."

Bev smiled, but couldn't help feeling a little guilty about their faith in her. But the debate wasn't meant to start for another ten minutes, so the spell would wear off in plenty of time.

Freddie considered the slice for a moment longer then finally took a very small bite.

Bev had to forcibly keep herself from exhaling. Was that enough?

"It's good. Did you get the blueberries from Herman? Or Alice?" He swallowed. "I'll have to thank them."

"Erm, Alice," Bev said, deciding not to mention that she'd gotten the lot from the bakers across the street. "You know, sometimes I get a wild hair to bake something other than rosemary bread. I'm glad you enjoyed it."

"Little lemony for my taste," he said. "But I appreciate it. I really hadn't had anything to eat all day."

"Weren't you having a campaign event?" Bev asked, looking at Petula.

"Indeed, but it was quite the busy afternoon," she said, licking her fingers. "Which explains our tardiness. Such a long walk. Can't say I really enjoyed it. I'm not meant to be traveling like this. I'm too old, you know?"

Bev swallowed her grimace as Petula covered her mouth in surprise and turned to Freddie and Gore.

"Erm, nice crowd, isn't it?" Bev said. "Lots of folks have come in. The inn was bustling again."

"We didn't pay for anything, did we?" Freddie said. "I swear, we don't have any gold left. Used all of it that we got from—"

"From contributions," Gore cut him off with a look. Before Bev could stop him, he took the rest of the bread from Freddie's hands. "I think that's enough sugar for you, Fred." He handed the bread back to Bev. "We've got to get ready for the debate."

Bev hid her disappointment. She'd wanted Gore to have a slice, too, but that ship had sailed. "Well, glad I could give you a little something, anyway. I've got to go find a seat before they're all taken."

"Bev," Petula said. "You're helping me with the questions, remember?"

Bev didn't want to tell her she'd already done so with the help of the lemon blueberry bread, so she feigned ignorance. "I am?"

"Yes, remember?" She cleared her throat, looking like she wanted Bev to recall something. "You're going to be asking the questions off the cards. And —ahem—add that one card we'd discussed earlier."

"What one?" Gore asked, narrowing his gaze.

"Erm. Just a standard question from the rules and regulations book," Petula said, with a little difficulty.

"I...don't think we need to ask it anymore," Bev said, with an eye on Gore.

Petula was going to ask why, but the clock in the tower chimed, and Petula jumped. "Time to start! Goodness, I get so antsy when things don't start on time. I feel like I'm letting everyone down." She covered her mouth. "Excuse me. Not sure where that came from."

Bev winced as they walked away. She hoped the magic faded quickly; otherwise, the whole town might learn more about the election monitor than they'd bargained for.

As Hendry, Freddie, and Wilda took their spots in the chairs lined up at the front of the room, Petula approached the crowd, holding up her hands to quiet the murmuring.

"Good evening, Pigsend," she said. "I'm elated to see such a large turnout for this very important event. You are all very keen on the future of your town, and as an election monitor, there's no greater joy in my life than seeing people conduct their civic duties." She cleared her throat, a move Bev was starting to sense was her realizing she was being a bit too truthful. "We are here tonight to hear from our three candidates. As you know, Mr. Norris had to unfortunately drop out after he received..." She shook her head, and Bev was grateful she'd stopped herself. "After he decided the race was too much for him. So our candidates this evening are Mayor Hendry."

Hendry rose and waved. Only a smattering of

applause, including from Bardoff and Rustin, could be heard.

"Ms. Wilda Murtagh."

Wilda stood, and there was more applause, but most of the room remained silent.

"And Mr. Freddie Silver."

Freddie came to his feet, and there was louder applause, but to Bev's eyes there weren't any more applauding for him than for Wilda. It really was anyone's race, and there were more than a few undecideds in the mix.

Petula smiled. "Wonderful. Now, tonight's event is a standard debate, as outlined in the official rule book. Bev has generously agreed to ask the questions, submitted anonymously from registered voters and posited to one of the candidates. That person will have one minute to answer, and, should a rebuttal be needed from another candidate, that candidate will also receive one minute." Her gaze landed on Lillie, who was sitting with Allen and the rest of Wilda's group. "*Only* registered voters are allowed to submit a question, so please be mindful of that."

Lillie shrank, shaking her head as if telling her she wasn't planning on saying a word.

"If anyone else has any questions, please submit them to Bev here." Petula gestured toward her. "Who, as you know, is the proprietor of the Weary Dragon. I'm not quite sure I can trust her, but there's no one else who—" She once again cleared her throat as her cheeks turned red. "Erm. Sorry. Bev?"

"Erm, right." Bev pulled the first one out of the crate. "This question is for…Wilda."

Wilda straightened with a satisfied smirk on her face.

"If elected, what do you plan to do about the limits on how much wheat we can sell in Middleburg?" Bev asked.

"What a lovely question," Wilda said, rising. "I want to thank whoever in the audience submitted that lovely question. Really, we have a town of such intelligent, thoughtful citizens. I know I'm lucky to count myself a member of Pigsend—"

"Answer the question, Wilda," Hendry muttered.

"I'm getting there, Jo, I'm getting there." Wilda turned to the audience and spoke in slow, halting words, pausing almost a little too much. "I want you to know that wheat selling remains at the forefront of my mind. Knowing that there are townsfolk struggling with it is very important to me. Wheat, after all, is such a big crop in Pigsend. It's the backbone of many of our industries, from the farmers who grow it, the miller who turns it into flour, and that flour that makes it into our baked goods all over town. I want you to know that anyone who brings me concerns will be absolutely listened to, unlike with the *current* mayor, who likes to kick people out of her office, and—"

"Time," Petula said, giving her a look. "Mayor Hendry, rebuttal? As a reminder to *all* candidates, your responses are limited to one minute each."

Hendry uncrossed her legs and looked down at the half-eaten blueberry bread still in her hands. Then, with a smirk at her opponents and at Bev, she shoved the rest of it in her mouth and rose to speak.

Chapter Seventeen

Bev's brows rose as Hendry approached the center of the room, taking her time and chewing thoughtfully. She swallowed hard, licking her lips and her fingers. Bev glanced at Petula, who was waiting with her timepiece poised, and realized the rebuttal only began when the candidate began speaking. Hendry was truly milking this for all it was worth.

But also…she knew exactly what the bread did. So why eat it right before speaking?

Hendry cleared her throat. "Good evening, fellow Pigsend citizens. I'm so pleased I have the opportunity to address all of you. Happy to shed light on this particular issue. The reason the regulations are the way they are is because they protect Her Majesty's farmers and ensure they profit the most. Which is her prerogative, of course. I've been lobbying our governor, who I have a *very* close relationship with, as you all know, to get them changed, but it's slow going. I can tell you that in the past two years, working with my *dear friend* Miranda, who we know is Wilda's cousin, I've been able to relax the requirement. Our farmers are now able to sell three wagons' worth instead of the one it had been."

Wilda scowled and glanced at Miranda in the audience, who glowered.

"And I *know* that's meant more gold in your and your *lovely* husband's pockets, Freddie. You primarily grow wheat, don't you?"

Freddie joined Wilda in scowling.

"But unfortunately, as mayor of Pigsend, one's hands are tied in many cases. But you know I do whatever I can to work within the system to get the best deal for all of us."

She sat, smiling out at the room. No one smiled back.

There was a long pause until Bev realized she needed to ask another question. She thumbed through the cards until she found one for Freddie, as he hadn't spoken yet.

"Freddie," Bev said. "You're a farmer who lives far out of town. Why should we choose you for mayor, when you don't have any experience?"

"What a great question," Freddie said, jumping to his feet. "I'm honored to be here, honored to share this stage with the other amazing candidates. This is a question I've been asked over and over again. It doesn't escape my notice that I'm the youngest up here by at least fifteen years—"

"*Ten*," Hendry said with a glare.

"And I know many of you wonder what a farmer like myself—a farmer who inherited his estate, no less—could bring to the table. Well, my friends, my pledge to you is that unlike *Hendry*, I don't take no for an answer. I plan on pushing those higher than me, people we haven't elected or chosen in any capacity, to be fairer in their decision making. It isn't right that one woman sitting hundreds of miles away can lord over the rest of us. When the king—"

"Time," Petula said. "And I would like to remind candidates to remain respectful toward Her Majesty."

Gore made a face at Freddie, and he sat, a little annoyed.

"Next question?" Petula prompted, but Hendry cleared her throat.

"I should be allowed to respond, correct?"

"Oh, right. Yes. Please. One minute, Mayor Hendry."

"I need half that," she said. "While I understand

the *fervor* Mr. Silver feels about how things have changed since the war, it's important that we remain clear-eyed about our present circumstances. And we must ask ourselves: do we want a mayor who marches in, sword and flag raised in attack, or do we want one who can get the job done?"

She waited, perhaps for applause, and when there was none, she narrowed her gaze.

"You ungrateful cretins," Hendry said. "You have *no* idea what sort of trouble I've kept out of town. The secrets I've kept about each and every one of you. You should be *grateful* that I'm your mayor, and—"

She stopped abruptly, opening and closing her mouth without a word as her cheeks turned pink. Then she sat with a huff. There was a noticeable shift in the crowd, as everyone looked at each other curiously.

"Bev?" Petula prompted. "One for Hendry, if you don't mind."

"She's answered two already," Wilda replied.

"She's *rebutted* two," Hendry said, throwing a lock of hair over her shoulder. "It's not my fault neither of you can keep my name out of your mouths."

Freddie and Wilda scowled.

"Right." Bev flipped through the cards quickly, but *every* question was for Wilda or Freddie. Finally, the mayor's name appeared on one of the cards, and

Bev began reading it without looking it over first.

"Mayor Hendry, why are you using your mind-control powers to win this election?"

Bev clamped her hands over her mouth and stared up at Hendry in horror. Hendry grimaced like she had a foul taste in her mouth, Freddie looked shocked and appalled, and Wilda smirked happily.

"You don't have to—" Bev began.

"No, I will *gladly* answer those accusations," she said. "Because there seems to be this prevailing belief that I've got mind-control powers. I don't. I merely use my powers of persuasion to get things done. Some of you may think that's a bad thing, but I see it as a valuable asset for a small-town mayor. There are people, including *certain people's cousins*, who think we're a backwater town with no need for a voice. They're here to see to it that Pigsend becomes even more eclipsed by larger towns in our midst. But I promise you that as your mayor, I've been fighting tooth and nail to make sure that doesn't happen." She cleared her throat. "When outside forces tried to ruin our Harvest Festival, who stepped up to make sure it stayed put?"

Me, Bev thought grumpily.

"And when soldiers installed a device that stopped magic in town, who made sure the real culprit was brought to justice?" Hendry continued.

Me, again. Bev glared at Hendry.

"Some might say our dear innkeeper," Hendry said, catching her gaze. "And to be sure, Bev had a large hand in solving the mysteries. But the consequences of those mysteries, making sure the outside forces didn't make good on their threats? That, dear friends, is the invisible work of your mayor. You'll notice we haven't seen Karolina or Claude or any other soldier who caused trouble in town again?"

Bev glanced around the room, seeing a smattering of begrudging nods from various people.

"Now, I can't promise that everything will always be roses, or I'll get what's best for us. But know that being your mayor means standing between you and the forces that would destroy this town. And I will always be that person."

"T-Time," Petula said, clearly enraptured. Bev wasn't even sure she'd been paying attention to the clock. "Erm. Next question?"

Bev continued to fish for cards and found no other surprises in the deck. She'd stuffed Hendry's card into her pocket, wanting to inspect it later. If the handwriting matched those of the letters then their blackmailer had shown up. One of the many faces in the crowd had more knowledge than they let on.

The debate continued rather uneventfully. Freddie or Wilda would be asked a question—

because there weren't any more for Hendry in the deck—but they'd inevitably mention Hendry, and she'd be allowed to respond. Wilda had been coached well by Miranda to give non-answers that sounded pleasing. Freddie veered a little too close to besmirching the queen but found a way to keep his temper. And Hendry's rebuttals were full of logical explanations for all the crimes levied against her administration. The truth-telling spell had worn off ages ago, but Hendry continued to speak as plainly and openly as she had under the influence.

Finally, at nine on the nose, Petula called for the debate to be over. There was a collective sigh from the candidates, all of whom had been tested with a wide range of questions, and from the crowd, who was tiring of the back-and-forth.

"One final announcement before you all leave," Petula said. "The election will officially begin at four o'clock tomorrow afternoon and run until midnight. Citizens will have their name checked on the official roll before casting their vote here at the town hall." She gazed out at the crowd, as if daring them to engage in any funny business. "I want to thank each of the candidates for coming this evening as well as the rest of you. I look forward to announcing the winner."

The audience rose and stretched, talking amongst themselves about the various answers the candidates gave and swapping town gossip. The candidates themselves quickly split to their respective supporter groups, presumably to be told how well they did. Hendry, with no such group, retired to her office, going to her desk and sitting down to work through papers as if it were ten in the morning.

"How did it go?" Lillie said, coming to Bev's side. "I saw Hendry eat her slice before she spoke. What was that about?"

"I haven't a clue," Bev said. "And I didn't get anything out of them. I don't think it's the candidates."

"Could still be Hendry," Lillie said. "Maybe she waited to eat the bread until she was on stage so you *couldn't* ask her about it."

"True," Bev said, watching the mayor in her office.

"I hear we have you to thank for that delicious bread, Lillie," Miranda said, walking over to join them. She wore a look that said she knew the two of them were up to something but wasn't exactly sure what it was. "I *must* borrow the recipe."

"It's Fernley's, Allen's mom's," Lillie said, her cheeks going pink. "And Bev made it. I didn't want anyone to think anything of it, you know? Since Wilda's my landlord."

"Mm. No one wants to think anything *suspicious* about the election, do we?" Miranda asked, looking directly at Bev. "Who in their right mind would want to sabotage a debate?"

"No one," Bev said pointedly. "But someone's sure keen on sabotaging the election. Perhaps to move a Harvest Festival to Middleburg?"

She made a face. "I didn't *say* that. And don't spread false rumors about my cousin, either. There are currently no plans to move the Pigsend Harvest Festival. Understand?" She spoke with such fervor that it was almost overcompensation.

Bev and Lillie shared a look then nodded in unison.

Miranda smiled and reached into her pocket. "In any case, this was delivered to me earlier today. Thought you might want to see it, being the assistant election monitor and all."

Bev unfolded the letter and frowned. It looked like the same handwriting as the letters Pip, Hans, and Wilda had received, but there was a new message.

> *If your cousin doesn't drop out before the debate, expect a visit from Dag Flanigan. He's already been summoned.*

"Who is—" Lillie began.

"He's a magic hunter," Bev said, trying to keep her face neutral. It was a good thing Pip had already dropped out—and an even better thing that PJ was in Sheepsburg. "Why would he have any reason to suspect Wilda? And do we have proof he's been summoned or is this an empty threat?"

"He's currently in Middleburg," Miranda said with a frown. "Or, at least, he was there when I left. Asked me to keep a close eye on things here and report back if I saw any mischief."

"And have you seen any?" Bev asked.

"Not that I'm willing to tell him about, no," Miranda said. "There are plenty of folks in Middleburg who skirt the line between what's allowed and what isn't, you know. Folks like Hendry, who might have a touch of magic, but not enough to attract Her Majesty's attention."

"But if Hendry has magic, why would she summon a magic hunter here?" Lillie asked pointedly. "Wouldn't that put her in danger, too?"

"Hendry's tangled with Mr. Flanigan twice," Miranda said. "I'm sure she's willing to try it a third time if it meant she could secure her seat."

"But Wilda's not dropping out, right?" Lillie said.

"Not right now, but she doesn't know about this letter." Miranda cleared her throat. "She did tell me about the first one but said it was election hijinks. I doubted *it* had any mention of Flanigan, did it?" She nodded to the letter in Bev's hand. "Go on, compare the handwriting with Hendry's only question. I bet they're identical."

Bev pulled out the card with Hendry's nasty

question and put it next to the letter Miranda had received. The handwriting was quite similar.

"I don't understand," Lillie said. "This question was awfully mean-spirited. Why would Hendry submit it herself?"

"Was it mean-spirited, or was it a well-placed question that allowed her to answer the primary grievances against her?" Miranda asked. "I know you and the mayor are *friends*, but you have to look at this objectively." She ticked off her fingers. "She keeps claiming she's going to win, but there's absolutely no evidence that she's anywhere near second place, even. The only people who want to vote for her are her own sheriff and that silly schoolteacher. She's obviously willing to move the election and not share information with her fellow candidates as long as it suits her." Miranda's brow raised. "Not to mention…*her list*."

"What list?" Bev asked.

"The list!" She laughed. "The one she's had since she was a little girl?"

Bev shook her head.

"Jo's *always* been a politician. Even when we were children, she was always learning whatever she could about people so she could use it against them. Kept it all written down in a little journal for easy reference. I can remember one time there was a boy who stole a pastry from Etheldra's tea shop—she was much younger, mind you, but still mean as a hornet. Somehow, Jo found out about it and made that poor boy do her homework for a whole year so she wouldn't tell on him."

"That's children being children," Bev said. "She's an adult now."

"Mark my words." Miranda pointed toward Hendry's open office. "Somewhere in that room, there's a list of everyone in Pigsend and their dirty little secrets."

Their conversation came to an abrupt halt when Petula came up, smiling thinly. Bev quickly hid the letter Miranda had given her in her pocket. "Well, other than that one hiccup, I think this went well. I couldn't help but notice, Bev, that you didn't ask any… What I mean is, the questions were, erm…" She glanced at Lillie. "Did you get the answers you were looking for?"

"Not exactly," Bev said, and Lillie took that opportunity to excuse herself. "But I'm convinced the three candidates aren't directly involved."

"I'm not sure what got into me at the outset," she said. "Must have been the exhaustion and the heat. But I kept feeling like I couldn't hold my tongue, you know?" She tittered. "In any case, did you happen to see who gave you that peculiar card?"

Bev shook her head.

"Hendry handled it well," Petula said. "But she's a professional."

That or she planted the card herself, as Miranda

had said.

Bev chewed her lip, looking around the room. Miranda's comment about Hendry's list weighed heavily on her mind. Hendry had given quite the speech about how much effort she put into the town. Perhaps she was trying to show off for the benefit of the crowd—though no one was paying attention to her.

"Suppose it'll all be over tomorrow," Petula said with a sigh. "Can't say I won't be happy when I can put this whole election behind me. It's too much like Modon for my liking. Next thing I know, I'll have an entirely new rumor spread about me." She chuckled. "Are you headed back to the inn?"

"Probably need to," Bev said.

"Mm." Petula's eyebrows wagged. "Is there, perhaps, a morsel of dinner still?"

"Oh yes, of course. I set aside a plate," Bev said. "I'll walk back with you. I've got a lot to do tonight."

And plenty to think about.

Chapter Eighteen

Petula gratefully took her cold dinner to the front room to eat and relax, and Bev set to scrubbing all the dishes while she thought about the night's events, especially all that Miranda had revealed. Now, it wasn't too far-fetched to think Miranda had written all the letters, including the nasty card to Hendry, and covered her tracks by writing another one. That was still a possibility. But she hadn't been in town when the first round was delivered, and Wilda had sworn her cousin didn't have a clue about her barus powers. Not to mention, how would Miranda know about PJ's powers? Or Hans's?

As much as Bev didn't want to agree with the

Middleburg mayor, it did seem most likely that Hendry was the culprit. She had the most to gain, she'd been in town long enough to know everyone's secrets, probably, and she wasn't above using them. While she'd insisted she hadn't used her so-called "mind control" powers to sway the election, what if that was a technicality? What if she'd used her powers to learn what she could, then included that information in the blackmail letters?

Bev sighed, looking down at Biscuit, who was watching her with wide eyes. "Suppose it would be too much to ask to make another loaf of bread and get her to eat it, eh?"

Biscuit sniffed.

"Yeah, you're probably right," Bev said.

The kitchen door swung open, and Petula walked in with an empty plate and a wide smile. "Here you go," Petula said. "Sorry to give you one more dish to wash."

"Happy to help," Bev said, taking it from her with a smile. "Hope it was good, even if it was cold."

"It was the best meal I've ever had," Petula said. "Though perhaps my opinion is changed by the fact that I hadn't eaten anything all day."

"I'm surprised Freddie didn't feed you," Bev said.

"They offered, of course, but I declined. I was already feeling strange accompanying him on his rounds, even if Ms. Murtagh and Mayor Hendry assured me they hadn't planned any events. It smacks of favoritism and..." She cleared her throat. "I must be tired."

"Mm." Bev was grateful no one else was around. "Well, I suppose I'll bid you a good night, so you can get your rest—"

Petula let out a breath. "You know, I'm a bit concerned about Mr. Silver, between you, me, and the walls. He's got a lot of, well, I don't want to call it rebellious ideas, but ideas that don't sit right with me. I worry what might happen if he actually gets elected." She paused. "Not for the town, really, but if he brings those ideas to the people higher up than him? The governors and such don't take kindly to that sort of talk. It wouldn't be a stretch for them to intercede and kick him out of office. Then, goodness, we're all right back where we started."

Bev chewed her lip. "Well, I'm sure he was glad to have you monitoring him. Did it seem like people were receptive to his ideas?"

"Hard to tell, sometimes, with farmers. They all had the same blank expression, you know?" She chuckled. "Do you perhaps have any more of that blueberry bread? It was absolutely scrumptious."

"No, but I can make some more tomorrow," Bev said. *Without the truth-telling magic.* "Have a good night, Petula."

She smiled, walked to the door, then stopped

and gasped. "Goodness, where did I put my rules and regulations book?"

"Oh." Bev crossed the kitchen to look into the front room. "I don't see it here. Did you bring it back with you?"

"It must still be at the town hall," Petula said with a sigh. "I wanted to brush up." She reached into her pocket and pulled out a set of keys on a ring. "Suppose I'd better head over and get it, hm?"

"Hendry gave you the keys to the town hall?" Bev asked.

Petula nodded. "Part of the protocol, you know. Don't want her sneaking in the night before to stuff the ballot boxes or anything like that. Not that she *would*, mind you, but all in the interest of propriety. Don't want to give any candidate access to the election space before it's time."

Bev was struck by an idea. "I'm happy to head over there and get it for you, if you like. You've been walking around all day, so I could just bring it up to you this evening."

Petula looked like she could've kissed Bev. "Really? Oh, Bev, that would be amazing. You really have such a good heart, helping me out like this. When I get back to Queen's Capital, I'm going to write a letter to the queen asking her to send you a medal for all the good work you do. You could hang it right next to your Harvest Festival ribbon."

Bev half-smiled. She wasn't sure how Freddie or

the others would take such a thing. "No letter necessary. Just happy to help."

And have an easy way to get into Hendry's office.

~

Bev stopped briefly to grab her glowing stick from the stables, earning her an annoyed bray from Sin for waking the old mule. Biscuit, ever curious, followed at her heel as she walked briskly toward the town hall. Even though Bev had a good reason for being out—and keys!—she still couldn't shake the feeling of guilt as she passed all the dark houses.

"I'm checking out what Miranda said," Bev muttered to herself. "I doubt Hendry has a list. She wouldn't be so...I mean, she probably knows everything about everyone, right? Doesn't have it written down."

Though as she thought about it, that was even worse.

"In any case, we'll find the book then take a quick peek."

She jogged up the steps to the town hall and fumbled with the keys until she found the right one. Inside, there was an echoing silence, and moonlight streamed through the windows. She swept the glowing stick along the benches, searching for Petula's book and finding nothing but unused question cards and a few peanut shells.

"Hm..."

Bev headed to the front of the room, where the candidate chairs remained. No book. She raised the glowing stick higher, scanning the walls and floors.

Biscuit let out a small *ruff*, catching Bev's attention. She turned until she found the laelaps, who was scratching at Hendry's closed door.

"Not yet, Biscuit, we have to find Petula's book first."

Biscuit, however, was insistent enough that Bev took notice. She'd learned long ago that for all the laziness and food-motivation of her trusty pet, he was quite intelligent, and whenever he scented something, she'd do well to follow.

Bev approached Hendry's door, a little surprised Hendry had given Petula *all* the keys, including to her office, but perhaps that was part of the protocol as well. Bev opened the door, wincing when it made a loud sound, before remembering she was alone here.

Biscuit bounded into the office, sniffing the floor, and Bev once again lifted her glowing stick to scan the room. There, on Hendry's desk, was Petula's book.

"Probably took it for safekeeping," Bev said, walking around to the other side of the desk and putting her hand on the book. She swept the glowing stick along the papers stacked neatly in piles. Every single one bore the queen's stamp, and had titles like *Security Protocol, Part II* and *Preferred*

Wine Types and Vintages, Part IV. Bev hadn't a clue what they meant, or why Hendry would have them. They didn't quite seem like things a mayor would be responsible for.

"What are you doing, Hendry?" Bev muttered, flipping through the papers.

More documents with the queen's stamp, more instructions on random things like regulations on cooking chicken and how many strawberries to serve. Bev only scanned their titles, as Petula would wonder what was taking so long if she didn't get back to the inn soon.

After searching through all the visible papers, Bev started opening drawers, looking for anything that might be a list of everyone in Pigsend. A notebook, a scroll, a ledger. Anything.

Biscuit was sniffing around too, and let out a yelp as he scratched at the lowest desk drawer. Bev opened it, finding more blank papers, but Biscuit was insistent. She lifted the stack until she found a small leather-bound notebook.

Bev chewed her lip, looking at the cover without opening it. Then she thumbed to the first page, which looked to be full of scattered notes and thoughts.

Daws, Etheldra. Relation to Witzel Butchers (see Ida), Dryad, Wife of Earl

> Dollman,
>   Born in Pigsend in ~~KT 1560~~ BQ 5,

"KT?" Bev said to herself. Then she realized this book had been written before the war, when the years were denoted by Kingstime instead of Before Queen, as they were currently listed. The BQ date was written in a much finer handwriting style, as Hendry must've updated the important dates when the Queen won the war.

> Bought the tea shop in KT May 1 from Gumble - deceased in 1585 KT
>   May 7 - threw me out of her shop for sass
>   May 9 - refused to sell me tea for my mother
>   May 10 - sent her an apology card. Tea acquired.

Bev chuckled, trying to calculate how old Hendry must've been when she'd written this. Eleven, perhaps? The entry continued, skipping a few months.

> August 10 - saw Frank Hamblin stealing a scone from her shop. <u>Have not told her</u>

That was a common refrain. Hendry had spent a lot of time in Etheldra's tea shop, which was the place of many observations. There were dalliances, arguments, the occasional handshake deal that wasn't exactly legal. All of it was well documented by a precocious child with a plan. But what was all this information for? Why would such a young child think to write all this down? Surely, she wasn't planning on being mayor when she was eleven years old.

Bev flipped to another entry, which was a lot less detailed.

> Dewey, Gore - Blacksmith, born in Pigsend. Brother Cornelius arrested by queen's soldiers for being a *kitsus*.

Bev stopped. What in the world was a *kitsus*?

Biscuit growled and scratched the floor, catching her attention. Right, she was supposed to be bringing Petula's book back to her. It had been almost a half-hour, and the election monitor would probably be wondering.

"Right, back to the inn." Bev replaced the floorboard and tucked Hendry's journal under her arm before hoisting Petula's heavy book with a grunt. No wonder the monitor was so tired, if she had to carry this thing around all day. "Let's get this to Petula."

Bev knocked on Petula's door three times, but the only sound was light snoring, so Bev placed the book against her door and left it there. Then she headed to her room with Biscuit and locked her door for good measure.

She placed Hendry's journal on her bed and found the loose floorboard where she hid her own assortment of illegal items, including a forbidden encyclopedia of magical creatures. She'd borrowed it during the sinkhole debacle, and Max the librarian had told her to keep it, as it was a little safer hidden at the inn than at the library. She'd referred to it a few times, though less so now that she had Merv and the wizard Percival to answer her magical questions.

It wasn't written in any particular order, so Bev had to scour it to find the creature listed as Gore's brother. It took her a bit, but finally she found the entry.

KITSUS

The kitsus is a creature of uncanny senses. Usually with large eyes, mouths, ears, nose, and

> mouth, the kitsus is known to have the enhanced abilities of sight, hearing, taste, and smell, more so than any normal person. Kitsus can smell a mouse from three miles away, and spot a rabbit on the other side of a forest while perched in a tree.

Bev eyed the creature depicted on the page. It was short, with round ears nearly the size of its head, and large, watery eyes that never blinked. The tongue was long and forked as it curled out of thick lips. The fingers, too, were long and spindly. The nose was permanently upturned, with the nostrils facing out instead of up.

"This was Gore's brother?" Bev muttered. "Half-brother, maybe?"

Bev looked back in Hendry's book, searching for mention of Gore's brother in his own entry but couldn't find it. Based on the way the pages came together, Hendry had unbound and rebound the journal multiple times. There were only entries for people who *currently* lived in Pigsend listed in the book, although there were clearly references to people who'd died or moved away. Vicky and Grant Hamblin were still listed, but their parents weren't.

Biscuit nudged her leg and stared at her.

"Right, we need to find the Norrises and

Wilda," Bev said. "And Hans."

Bev returned to the journal, flipping through quickly until she found Pip Norris's entry. It was quite small, containing only his name, occupation, birthday, wedding day to Holly, PJ's birthday, and a listing of his current clients. There were a few incidents, some from when he was younger, some more recent, but one entry did give her pause

> 10 February - Son PJ possible suspect in Earl Dollman's warehouse collapse. _Still no resolution to this._ (Ask Bev)

Bev stared at that a few times, harkening back to that episode. Hendry _had_ intimated that she thought PJ and his friends were guilty—not because he was a dragon shifter, but because they were teens with too little to do.

She flipped the page, finding Holly's entry next with much of the same information. Then PJ's entry, with a separate note that he'd moved to Sheepsburg. But absolutely no mention of the younger Norris sprouting wings or spewing fire.

Bev flipped back to the Murtaghs, which she'd scanned quickly but hadn't read in detail. Wilda and Lazlo were mentioned, as was Miranda (Bev supposed the Middleburg mayor was the exception to the "only people in Pigsend" rule). There were paragraphs about all of them, slights and secrets, the Harvest Festival kerfuffle, mention of the barus bauble Bev had found in the pie, but not where it had come from.

Next, she checked the journal for Freddie and Hans. Theirs was scant—birthdays, their wedding date, some important ideas. What appeared to be a fresh note about Freddie running for mayor, and a reminder to dig up more dirt about him. But no mention of Hans's magic.

Bev sat back in her bed, looking out the dark window. Obviously, this journal was important to Hendry, and she kept it updated regularly, at least since Earl's warehouse collapse. The Witzels' entries bore the details about Ida's magic, and of course, Etheldra's was clear to name her as a descendent of dryads as well. Bathilda Wormwood's entry mentioned the tanddaes (which Bev had known Hendry had known about). There were all manner of incriminating secrets—including magical abilities —but the three secrets revealed during this campaign were oddly missing.

Did that mean Hendry didn't write them down, perhaps sensing she might be found out? Or did she really not know?

Bev's eyelids grew heavy, but she kept flipping through the pages until she reached the end. There was a single entry there, and to Bev's estimation, there should've been much more detail included than was written down. Still, the information was somewhat enlightening:

Bev (no last name)

~~Beverage Wench at~~ Weary Dragon Inn since 1AQ - Owner since 3AQ

Figured out the sinkholes, friend of the moleman

<u>Keep on good side.</u>

Chapter Nineteen

The morning of the election dawned gray and overcast, which at least meant a break from the heat. Bev fed Sin and Biscuit and swept the front room, even though she'd already swept it the night before. Anything to keep from having to sit still and think about the election.

At a quarter to seven, the front door opened, and Bev turned, expecting Allen or Lillie with the baked goods early. Instead, it was Mayor Hendry, dressed in a striking emerald tunic that went well with her dark hair and blood red lips. She didn't look happy to see Bev, forcing a neutral smile.

"Good morning," she said, as if unsure what to make of Bev standing with her broom in the front room. "I see you were in my office last night."

"I'm sorry?" Bev asked, quirking her brow.

"Petula had left her rules and regulations book at the town hall," Hendry said, gesturing to the empty tables. "I put it in my office under lock and key. This morning, it was missing. My office door was unlocked. And there was a particular shade of golden dog fur on my floor." She quirked a brow. "Ergo…"

"Ah, yes. Petula asked me to get it for her," Bev said, relaxing a little. "She was so tired after the day and didn't want to walk all the way back over there. She had keys. I believe you gave them to her." Bev paused. "So sorry about not locking back up. Suppose my mind was elsewhere. And for Biscuit shedding. I know you aren't a fan of his."

"Mm." Hendry eyed her. Did she know her journal was missing? "Well, I'm glad her property was returned to her, even though I'd planned to do it myself this morning so I could speak with her before the election."

"What about?" Bev asked.

"None of your concern, Bev," she said. "Just some last-minute election things to take care of. Even if it may be my last day in office." She inhaled and exhaled, sizing up the Weary Dragon as if it were a piece of the domain she was about to part with. "I'm not counting my chickens before they're hatched, but I'm not quite as confident as I was yesterday."

"What's changed?" Bev asked. "Did you…get a letter?"

"No, Bev, I didn't get a letter." She snorted. "I have eyes. I have ears. And unless something rather large changes between now and when they count the votes, I'm pretty sure I'm *not* going to win."

Bev tilted her head. "I'm sorry to hear that. You've been a…well, you've been a good mayor in my book. Even though you've asked a little too much of me at times."

"Oh, please, you were more than willing to help," Hendry said with a sad smile.

"Still." Bev smiled. "You should stick around a few minutes. Allen will be bringing the muffins by. At least you can start the day with something sweet. Lighten the mood."

"I assume there won't be any magic in these confections?" Hendry asked.

Bev cleared her throat. "What do you mean?"

"Well, in this case, I meant your little parlor trick of spiking the blueberry lemon bread with whatever kind of magic it was," Hendry said. "But generally, we've noticed that Mr. Mackey's baking has taken a delicious turn for the better. One might say a magical turn, and I don't believe it's Lillie's doing, either."

Bev pursed her lips. She hadn't even thought to see if Hendry knew Lillie's secrets. "Perhaps he's learned a thing or two from her."

"Bev, come now, we've been through far too much to beat around the bush," Hendry said. "Allen's got his mother's magic, finally, and I know you have my journal." She extended her hand. "I want it back, please. There are things in there that shouldn't be seen by certain folk, if you catch my meaning."

Bev was caught off guard by the sudden topic change, but after a moment, she found the journal, which she'd stashed under her guest book to keep close at hand, and slid it over to Hendry.

"I hope you found it enlightening," Hendry said softly. "I told you, I'm innocent. If anything, I'm a *victim* here. Someone's trying to frame me."

"I will say that nothing in the letters was found in your journal," Bev said, being careful with her words. "But it's not the most innocent-*looking* thing to have, you know. There's a lot of Pigsend's dirty laundry in that book."

"Which is why I keep it hidden," Hendry said. "I don't relish keeping it, but in my line of work, one never knows who's hiding something strange. Especially since the war, when everyone had to hide who and what they were. But even before then, people didn't take too kindly to those with overt magic. The only folks who really fit in were those like Fernley and Ida, who could pass as a bit quirky." Hendry stopped and swallowed. "Someone with the ability to sway people and convince them of things…let's say I didn't make many friends growing up. Well," she chuckled, "willingly."

"So you gathered secrets on people so they wouldn't spill yours?" Bev asked softly.

"And became mayor so I could keep one step ahead of Her Majesty," Hendry said. "Know exactly when the soldiers would be arriving and how many. Of course, I've been surprised a few times here and there—notably with Allen's father at his wedding—but on the whole, it's been…well, it's how I've kept myself safe." She shuddered. "Not sure what I'm going to do tomorrow when I haven't a clue what's coming."

"You're a brilliant woman," Bev said. "I'm sure you'll figure it out."

"I could say the same for you," Hendry said. "But I suppose you still throwing darts at the wall means you haven't figured out who's trying to sabotage the election?"

Bev shook her head. "Everyone has a motive, and no one's dropping out."

"Suppose it doesn't matter. They failed. The election's going to happen however it's going to happen. If the blackmailer's candidate wins, that's that." She ran her finger along the front desk. "It seems everyone has a vested interest in staying in."

"What do you mean?" Bev asked.

"Well, they're theories, of course." Hendry

smiled as if they weren't. "I believe Wilda's running so her cousin can move the Harvest Festival. Miranda's always been the bully in that family, and does whatever she wants to get her way. She wasn't too happy her plans were ruined last year, and Miranda's nothing if not determined."

"And Freddie?" Bev asked.

"You know, I honestly can't say for sure. I was really quite surprised when I found out. He's such a staunch proponent of the kingside—or was, I should say. There really isn't a kingside anymore." She shook her head. "Gore, too, doesn't seem the kind who'd want to throw his lot in with a mayor who swears allegiance to the queen."

"Maybe they're planning to, I don't know, not swear allegiance," Bev said, recalling what Petula had said.

"Good luck with that." Hendry laughed. "They'll be wrapped up in irons before they can say a word against her. All that work, to be thrown in jail." She shrugged. "I can't say it's worth it, but what do I know?"

"And you're in to save your own skin," Bev said.

"Well, I do enjoy the work." She smiled. "I love Pigsend. I love the people, the quiet way of life. I even love Etheldra, if you can believe it. Everyone's got their own quirks, but it's a wonderful little village. And honestly, the best part of my job is when I can affect change without anyone being the wiser." She looked around as the clock struck seven. "If you see Petula, please let her know I'm looking for her. I do have a few things to take care of this morning, before I'm summarily kicked out of office. I'm sorry to have missed those delicious, magic-laced muffins."

Bev furrowed her brow. "I don't think Allen knows he's still got magic, by the way."

"You don't think so?" Hendry asked.

"He hasn't mentioned anything to us, and he's not taking care with his baking the way—" Bev caught herself. "The way he should. But I think he's the only one who still has their magic after the madness at the solstice."

"That is curious." Hendry furrowed her brow. "I suppose it has been long enough, Allen's probably got it for good, don't you think?" She lifted her shoulder. "Might be worthwhile to tell him. Just so he can be on his guard in case any magic hunters waltz through town again."

Just then, the front door opened, and Allen arrived carrying his basket of muffins. He stopped short at seeing Hendry then gave her an awkward wave.

"M-morning." He lifted the basket. "Muffin?"

"Don't mind if I do." Hendry sauntered by him and plucked one off the top. "Lemon blueberry?"

"Yeah, got inspired by Bev last night," Allen said with a chuckle.

"I'm *sure* you did," Hendry said, giving Bev a sideways glare. "I suppose I'll see you at the town hall later, Allen? After the poll results come in, I hope we can continue to be friends, even after you supported my nemesis and her cousin."

"I hope so, too." Allen smiled at her. "Good luck, Mayor Hendry. I hope…well, I hope today treats you well."

"Ah, Mayor Hendry. Suppose everyone will have to start calling me *Jo* again." She hummed to herself as she walked out the door.

"What was *that* about?" Allen said, hurrying over to Bev. "What was she doing here? Trying to kidnap Petula so she'd let her win?"

"Petula left her rule book at the town hall last night. Hendry was dropping it off," Bev said, opting for something close to the truth. "She's pretty down about her chances of winning today."

"Glad it's finally sunk in for her. I was starting to wonder if she was delusional." Allen chuckled, glancing up the stairs. "Has Petula made it down yet?"

"Not yet. But I'm sure she'll be here in a minute. Lots to do today." Bev picked up a muffin, immediately sensing the zing of magic. "Lillie off this morning?"

"Yeah. We're pretty much closed after I deliver these," Allen said. "Besides baking more for Wilda, of course. She wants to do some last-minute canvassing to make sure all our voters come out." He paused. "Why? Is there something wrong with them?"

Hendry's warning sat uncomfortably in her stomach, and she couldn't help but agree with her. It had been over a month since the solstice. Perhaps time to let Allen know he was unwittingly infusing magic into his goods, especially as people were clearly hoarding secrets.

"Allen, I…have to tell you something," Bev began slowly. "About your…well, about your baking."

"Don't tell me you're not a fan anymore," Allen said, his eyes widening. "Or you don't want me to bring you morning pastries. Oh, Bev, I do love our morning chats. It's my favorite part of the day, Lillie's too, and—"

"It's not that," Bev said. "It's that…well, since the solstice…"

"I've had pobyd magic?" Allen asked with a relieved smile.

Bev blinked at him. "How did you—?"

He chuckled. "You really thought I hadn't noticed? Bev, I'm practically oozing magic into everything I touch. Well," he shook his head as he picked up a muffin, "to be fair, I *didn't* notice until after the magical river subsided. But when it did, and I realized the magic in the flour was coming from me…"

"So you've known all this time?" Bev said, laughing. "Why didn't you say anything to Lillie or me?"

"Well, to be honest, I was wondering when *you* would mention it," he said, a little cheekily. "I mean, I know we've been busy with the election, but I *also* know Lillie's been sucking the magic from my baked goods before they go out. Which, I do appreciate, as you never know who's going to be coming into town. But I suppose I was waiting to see who would blink first."

"I don't know about blinking, but," Bev settled on her stool, smiling at him fondly, "I was trying to spare you some heartbreak. In case the magic disappeared. I know you miss your mother terribly, and you were so keen to have her close again."

"You thought it would disappear?" Allen said. "Why?"

"Well, everyone else's did," Bev said. "I do wonder why yours didn't."

He considered the muffins for a moment. "I think I've always had it. But I never really noticed it was there until the solstice. Then it was very pronounced. I couldn't avoid it if I tried. When all the excess magic disappeared, all that was left was this little flicker." He smiled. "I'm obviously nowhere near as skilled as Lillie, but enough to get on with. It feels like my mother is back with me, too. Which is a good thing, because Vicky took her engagement ring with the pobyd bauble with her to Sheepsburg. She says she doesn't need it, but I think she's hanging onto it on the off chance..." His cheeks reddened. "In any case, I think my magic is here to stay."

Bev patted his hand. "Lillie and I are so happy for you."

"Yes, you're quite the duo these days," Allen said with a laugh. "I'll be sure to tell her she can stop inspecting everything I bake now. She's not as discreet as she thinks she is."

"I'd let her keep at it," Bev said. "If you can't stop yourself from infusing magic into your pastries."

He picked up a muffin and considered it. "I'll have to get Lillie to tell me how to fix them. Make them perfectly delicious instead of absolutely scrumptious, you know?"

"Is there a difference?" Bev laughed.

"Maybe. She's the expert." He grinned then his face fell when he glanced at the clock. "Duty calls. Etheldra will be furious if I'm late delivering her mini-pies this morning, and Wilda expects us all to be at her house by nine to start canvassing. It's going to be a long day."

Bev gazed at the muffins. The only folks who'd rented rooms were farmers who'd stayed too late after the debate the night before, but she was still nervous handing these out. "Maybe you should bring these to Lillie and have her tweak them. They're quite potent."

He frowned. "Bev, they're fine. It's not *that* much magic. My mother had no problem baking and selling goods."

"Yes, but your mother didn't have to worry about soldiers staying across the street every couple of weeks, eating your breakfast pastries," Bev said with a shake of her head. "Besides, I daresay you might have *more* than she did. At least, I don't recall feeling the magic in her muffins as acutely as I do in yours." She pushed the basket back toward him. "You can bring them back. I'm sure it won't take her any time at all."

"Fine, fine." He sighed. "You know, it would be lovely if the queen's soldiers would find some other village to terrorize. Maybe I'll ask my father if he can pull some strings next time he stops in."

"Did he say if he was planning on visiting again?" Bev asked.

"No, but you know him. Likes to pop up whenever. Like Dag Flanigan." He shook his head. "I don't know what they all find so fascinating about Pigsend. But at least, since the solstice, we haven't seen a single—"

The front door to the inn opened and the magic hunter himself strolled in with a wide smirk.

Chapter Twenty

Allen carefully slid the basket back toward himself. "You know, I think you're right, Bev. These need a few minutes more in the oven. Can't imagine where my head is today."

With that, he hurried toward the door, sliding around the queen's soldier without meeting his gaze. The soldier didn't notice the baker, his dark eyes fixed on Bev. With the large scar down his cheek, he was an imposing figure. He always knew more than he should've about what went on in Pigsend. He scanned the room, as if looking for someone magical to arrest on the spot, before approaching Bev.

"Good to see you again, Bev," Flanigan said. "I hear things have been…interesting in Pigsend lately."

"No more than usual," Bev replied, and to be fair, it was the truth. "We're having a little mayoral election today, which is the cause of all the activity. You may see a few more people in town, as everyone will be coming in to vote later."

"Is that all you have to report?" He stood in front of her, as if expecting her to say something else. When she didn't, he sniffed and reached into his pocket, pulling out a letter. Bev's stomach dropped as he unfolded it and placed it on the counter then slid it over toward her.

> Mr. Flanigan,
> I think you'll find something interesting in Pigsend. You should speak to each candidate running for mayor. They're all hiding something.

"Well, that's certainly a letter," Bev said, unable to think of anything else to say. "What do you think it means?"

"I don't know. But it intrigued me enough to make the trip." He cracked a smile at her. "This town's been something of a sore spot with me since I let that dang dragon shifter escape. I've still got questions for those old women if I ever see them again."

"The grannies?" Bev chuckled. "Oh, they're

harmless. Bit quirky, though. Poor dears."

Also dragon shifters, but Dag didn't need to know that.

"I feel like there's something you aren't telling me, Bev," he said.

She got the unnerving sensation that he could see right through her. If he didn't hunt down magical people, she would've sworn he had magic himself.

"You're not the only one who received a nasty letter like that," Bev said, after a moment. "Every candidate but Mayor Hendry got one, too. Not sure what they were about, of course, but then, most people have secrets."

"Usually, people's secrets don't bother me unless they're of a specific kind," Flanigan said. "So which candidate has magic, Bev?"

All of them? Bev shook her head, hoping she didn't look guilty. "I don't know. A case could also be made that someone was taking advantage of your presence. You tend to make people uneasy, on account of your reputation."

"Mm." He surveyed her. "As I recall, someone was trying to make me the bad guy the first time I was in town."

"What do you mean?"

"I recall that Bernie fellow, the one I arrested for illegal use of magic, had been threatening the butchers across the street with something or another," he said. "Wasn't it about a registration?"

Bev nodded. "Yes, but he was lying about it. She's been keeping up with her paperwork dutifully."

"Yeah, well, he's not lying to anyone at the moment, not after I saw him using that ring." Dag cracked a wry grin, and Bev didn't want to think about where Bernie might be. "You know, I crossed paths with Zed Mackey recently. I understand you're well acquainted with him now."

"Yes, he spent a few weeks here. I hear he's your boss." Bev nodded to the door. "His son, who just left, was going to get married, but it didn't work out."

"Then there was the summer solstice," Dag continued. "Lots of strange activity then, he said."

Bev made a noncommittal noise. How much had Zed told his magic-hunting subordinate? She hoped he'd spared some of the more sordid details, such as giant chickens and houses sprouting into flowers, especially as Zed himself had been changed into a gingerbread man, and needed Bev and her friends to change him back.

"Well, since I'm here, might as well speak with the candidates," he said, almost lazily. "Who all is running?"

"Hendry, of course," Bev said. "Wilda Murtagh and Freddie Silver. Ms. Petula Banks is our election monitor and she'd be happy to point you in the right direction." Bev paused. "I don't think you'll find anything amiss, though."

"No, but it's as you said." He chuckled. "My presence makes people uneasy. Uneasy people make mistakes."

Bev didn't doubt that Flanigan's presence would cause a stir, but when she finally made it out to the town square for the festivities, no one was talking about it. Everyone was abuzz with election excitement, especially as the two larger campaigns had reclaimed their spaces they'd had during the question-and-answer session and had once again called upon their campaign supporters to convince people through their stomachs.

Freddie, Ida, and Vellora were distributing the sausage and potato, and Hans was monitoring the pig over the fire pit. None of them looked even remotely worried; in fact, even Hans was proudly standing next to his husband with a grin on his face.

Across the town square, Wilda gleefully handed out cupcakes with the bakers, none of whom looked worried, either. Bev walked toward them slowly, looking around the town square for signs of Flanigan. But when she spotted Miranda standing off to the side, she turned on her heel and marched over.

"Flanigan is here, as you predicted," Bev said. "Does your candidate know?"

"I didn't predict anything. I got a letter saying he would be summoned. I knew he was nearby. That's all." Miranda gave Bev a look. "Don't tell me you still think it's *me*."

"I'm saying it's suspicious."

"Hendry has as much knowledge of the soldiers' locations as I do." Miranda nodded to Hendry, who was greeting people as they walked into the town square. "She probably also knew Flanigan was close. But unlike me, she didn't deign to tell you. You should probably go ask her about it." She smirked. "Goodness knows she's not *busy* or anything."

Bev turned to Hendry again. Although the mayor was trying to engage with everyone who walked by, everyone seemed to be giving her a wide berth after nodding their hellos.

"Flanigan said he was going to speak with all the candidates," Bev said. "Has he come to talk with Wilda yet?"

"Not to my knowledge," Miranda said. "But if he does come by, there's nothing to tell him, other than he needs to speak at length with Hendry. Which is what I suggest you do, as well."

As if proving a point, Miranda walked away. Bev waited a minute before crossing the square to ask Hendry about Flanigan.

"I get reports of soldiers' comings and goings," Hendry said, trying to shake a passing farmer's hand to no avail. "I got a notice he was in the area, but I didn't expect him to come here."

And clearly, Flanigan hadn't made good on his threat to interview each candidate. "Did anyone *else* know Flanigan was in Middleburg?" Bev asked, tiredly.

Hendry glared at Miranda across the square. "Miranda, presumably."

"Yes, she told me." Bev was feeling the beginnings of a headache coming on. "But Miranda also received a letter stating if her cousin didn't drop out, they'd summon Flanigan. Well, here Flanigan is, so—"

"And I bet you ten gold coins she wrote that letter herself to throw you off the scent." She gestured toward Miranda. "Well? Go on. Bother her. I've got to work the square. Can't leave anything to chance this close to the election."

Bev didn't cross the square back to Miranda; instead, she walked into the town hall and sat on one of the benches. Petula sat at a table in the front of the room, monitoring voters as they came and went. Each voter took a card and walked to one of two corners with a small desk facing the wall. They'd write down their vote, then return the card to Petula, who'd slip it into a box.

The queue was steady and moving, but once people cast their vote, they found their friends in the crowd and stood around to catch up. No one was in a hurry to leave, as everyone was eager to find out the results of the election.

Bev let out a breath. She was honestly about ready to give up on this whole endeavor. The election was going to be over soon, and whoever had the secrets would presumably keep holding onto them. After all, what good was pressuring Wilda or Freddie to drop out if things were over?

She rose, ready to hit the candidates again with questions they probably wouldn't have answers to, when she stopped suddenly. Valta Climber was out front, along with her parents, who were talking with Earl and Jane Medlam, the mason. Valta looked bored out of her mind, as she was too young to vote and presumably uninterested in anything related to the election. But she might have an answer to one of Bev's burning questions.

"Hey, Valta!" Bev called.

The teenager smiled as she spotted Bev and waved happily, jogging over after speaking with her parents. Bev waved hello to the Climbers, who she didn't know all that well, and nodded to Valta.

"How are you? Been a while since I've seen you in town."

"I've been put on a pretty tight leash," she said with a scowl. "My folks were overjoyed when they heard Grant and PJ were skipping town. Of course, they wouldn't hear *a word* of me going with them. But I did get them to agree that if I helped on the farm and did all my chores without complaint for the whole summer, they'd let me go visit during the solstice." She looked excited by that idea. "Can't wait. Solstice in Sheepsburg. I'm sure it's much more exciting than here."

"Just be sure you come home after," Bev said with a laugh.

"Don't tempt me. I already got three letters from PJ telling me how *amazing* it is. Grant's got a nice apartment, furnished by his aunt, who he doesn't hate anymore because she's giving him a ton of money, and—"

"Actually, Valta, I had a question for you," Bev said, cutting her off. "About PJ. And his...well..."

"Yeah, I saw that Flanigan guy when we arrived," Valta said. "He's on the outskirts of town watching everyone who comes and goes like they're guilty. Don't tell me he's here looking for the, erm..." She gestured to the air. "You know."

"Not here." Bev looked around. "C'mon."

Valta nodded, a crease forming between her brows, as she followed Bev out of the town hall. It was hard to find a private spot, as there were people milling about everywhere, but they rounded a corner and leaned in to speak quietly.

Bev told her briefly about what had happened, starting with the specific letter to Pip about PJ.

Valta shook her head, shocked. "There's no way," she said. "Nobody knew except PJ's family, me, and Grant, and he wouldn't tell a soul. I don't know how someone found out. We've all been so careful with it, you know?"

"I know," Bev said. "There are other secrets, too. Ones nobody's supposed to know that somehow this *one* person does. I can't square how it happened. It seems too coincidental, almost."

"I mean, Mayor Hendry probably did it," Valta said. "I heard my mom talking once about how she's got mind-control powers."

"It's not her." Bev paused. "At least, I'm pretty sure it's not her."

"You said everyone got a letter but her, right?"

"Yeah."

"I mean…" Valta made a face then thought better of it. "Well, if I were to pick someone *other* than Hendry, I'd probably pick Gore. He's kinda intense. He showed up at the house the other day promising all kinds of stuff if my parents voted for Freddie. Kinda insinuated that they owed him, considering he spent all that time on Gilda and she left for Silverkeep. I can't imagine Freddie winning means all that much, but apparently it does."

Bev nodded slowly. "I'm going to go have a chat with him and see what I can find out." She smiled. "Thanks, Valta. If you get out to Sheepsburg, tell PJ and Grant I said hello. I do miss seeing them—and you, too."

She beamed. "Nice to be missed. Maybe I'll get lucky, and my parents will let me visit Gilda in

Silverkeep, too."

"Maybe so."

~

It wasn't the first time Gore had appeared on Bev's suspect list, nor did she think it was damning that he'd threatened the Climbers into voting for Freddie. There had been a lot of that sort of pressure going around, for sure. But it still raised some questions in her mind, and she was keen to get them answered.

She glanced at the darkening sky. The competing smells of sugar and spice were a bit jarring, but were reflective of the two candidates.

Three, Bev reminded herself mildly.

She didn't see Gore, but Hans was working the crowd with a smile on his face. He waved at Bev as she approached, and offered her a slice of chicken off a nearby tray.

"Did you vote yet?" he asked.

"Not quite yet," Bev said. "Is Gore around?"

"He's off with Freddie," Hans said. "Why? What's wrong?"

Bev looked around, then motioned for Hans to follow her around the corner of the schoolhouse. "Did you guys get another letter?"

"No, but we got a visit from Dag Flanigan." Hans's face darkened. "He said he wanted to speak with Fred, so they've gone off to talk in private, and Gore went with them." He shivered. "Don't know what the heck he's doing in town."

"Someone invited him," Bev said. "Whoever's been sending the letters. Have you told Freddie about yours yet?"

He shook his head. "Gore still didn't want me to. But you know him—he's so keen on winning."

"And why is that?" Bev asked. "I mean, obviously he wants Freddie to win, but…why?"

"Honestly, I don't know. I don't even know why Freddie wanted to run," Hans said, looking around as if he were worried he'd be overheard. "He's always liked politics and all that, but… I've never heard him once mention he wanted to be mayor. Just kind of random."

Bev nodded. "If Gore's so interested in winning, why didn't he run himself?"

"You'll have to ask him that," Hans said. "I know he's always been sore about the queen being in power, and I know his brother was taken away right after the queen won. Apparently, he had some kind of very dangerous magic."

"Really?" And Gore didn't have it? "What kind?"

Hans thought for a minute. "Fred said it was the kind that could get a person in trouble. Not a wizard or mage magic like mine, but perhaps *more* dangerous, because of what it was." He shook his head. "He wouldn't tell me more than that, though."

Bev thought back to the journal, and the entry in her encyclopedia. "A kitsus, I think it was, right?"

"Oh, a kitsus?" He shook his head. "I mean, I could see that. Kitsus are known for having super senses. Probably could smell us a mile away."

Bev stopped and looked at him, something clicking in her mind. "Would they be able to overhear something, too?"

"Probably, I—"

"Fire! Fire! Everybody out!"

Bev and Hans shared a look then scrambled back to the town square. Smoke filled the air, but it wasn't coming from the Witzels' fire pit.

It was coming from the town hall.

Chapter Twenty~One

It took Bev a moment to realize what was happening, but it was Hendry's clear voice that snapped her to attention.

"Everyone out of the town hall," she said, walking through the crowd like a general commanding an army. "Earl, fetch the pails. I want everyone standing next to one another, to the creek. We've done this before. Hurry, hurry."

Everyone did as she said. Whether it was Hendry's magic or that people were worried about the town hall, Bev didn't know, but she queued up between Bardoff and Alice to move pails of water from the creek on the other side of town, to the town hall. Lucky for the building, there were plenty of folks in town, and once it was clear what was going on, everyone pitched in to help.

"Don't just stand there, Freddie," Hendry said, snapping at her competition, who was, indeed, standing and watching smoke pour out of the town hall. "Hop to it. Grab a pail."

Freddie jumped, surprised Hendry had spoken to him, then joined the queue, his face a bright red color. Hendry walked up and down the line, overseeing the water transfer. Every so often, she'd take an empty pail from someone so a full one could keep moving toward the burning building. All the while, her encouraging voice echoed in the crowd.

"That's it, one right after the other," she said, walking by Bev. "Pick up the pace, Wilda. Try not to spill so much."

Wilda scowled as she heaved the full pail of water to Lillie, who passed it on to Allen, and on down the line.

"How's it looking?" Bev asked as Hendry walked by.

"We're fighting the good fight. I think it's mostly contained, but we need to make sure." She turned toward the building, brow furrowed. "I'd hate to see the thing go up in flames."

"Any idea what started it?" Bev said.

"We'll figure all that out once the fire is out," Hendry said, her lips pressed into a thin line. "I don't think whoever's sabotaging the election is happy with their polling results. Want to give themselves another day."

Bev glanced down the line, to where Hans stood with the butchers. Gore was nowhere to be seen, though Freddie had managed to find a spot right next to the building.

The water pails continued back and forth, until finally—thankfully—Hendry announced that the fire was out. A loud cheer rose from the crowd as everyone left the orderly line, clapping each other on the back and shaking hands. The scent of burning wood was still thick in the air, but no more smoke came out of the front doors.

Inside, the floors were slick from the water, but all the burning was contained to a single corner— one where voters had been casting ballots. Petula stood at the back of the room, the ballot box clutched in her hand as if it were a sacred item. She was deep in conversation with Dag, whose eyes had narrowed in concentration.

"Ah, Bev," Petula said, waving her over. "I'm so glad you're here. I was telling Mr. Flanigan about all the mishaps we've had at this election. Bev has been instrumental in helping me keep an eye on things."

Flanigan looked at the burnt spot in the corner and raised his brows at Bev. "Doesn't look like you did a good job of that tonight."

"Did anyone see how the fire started?" Bev asked.

Petula shook her head. "I was collecting ballots, and I smelled smoke. I looked up and saw the corner on fire. Immediately told everyone to evacuate. Hendry said she'd take it from there."

Bev crossed the room and knelt by the burnt wood. It was still warm but no longer aflame. Biscuit was back at the inn, or else she would've asked him to come sniff for any signs of magic. There was something about the quickness of the spread that gave her pause. The town hall was made of wood, of course, but—

"Oh, good, the votes are still safe," Wilda said, walking into the building with Miranda in tow. "Are we going to restart the vote or—"

"I don't think that's wise," Hendry said, coming in after her. "The townsfolk have been shaken up. Some of them went home without casting a vote. We've got to make sure it's fair for everyone."

"You're only saying that because you think demonstrating a *small* amount of leadership changed some votes for you," Freddie said, walking in behind her.

"I didn't see *you* winning any votes, gaping like a fish as you were," Hendry said before leveling her gaze at Gore. "And you, where in the world did *you* go? I daresay I'd say you're the one who started it, Gore. You work with fire enough—"

"Oh, come off it. We know you started it," Wilda snapped. "Trying to buy yourself more time and votes. Hendry swoops in to save the day after yet another calamity befalls Pigsend."

"How in the world did I start the fire when I wasn't even in the room?" Hendry said. "Clearly, it was one of your subordinates." She gazed at Miranda. "Or family."

"Don't look at me," Miranda said. "But I do find it just charming that you have to have everyone in town band together to get water. In Middleburg, we have a fire brigade that—"

"*Enough*!" Petula cried, causing all three candidates to abruptly stop talking. "I have had *enough* of the sniping and the griping and the rude remarks. All of you, *to the inn*. We are going to have a long and detailed *chat*."

"I think I'd like to come with you," Dag drawled. "Might find something interesting."

"*You* stay here," Petula said. "Work with Rustin to keep an eye on the people and make sure nothing else goes up in flames. If there's something to tell you, I will be sure to do it. Now." She turned to the candidates. "*March*."

~

No one said a word on the short walk back to the inn. Bev kept sneaking glances at Gore, who trailed behind Freddie until Petula snapped her fingers at him to keep up. Bev opened the front door to the inn and let everyone walk through. Biscuit, who'd been snoozing at the hearth, perked up and wagged his tail, though even he read the room and sank back down.

"Find a seat," Petula said, pointing to the tables.

Everyone did as instructed, though Bev went to sit on her stool behind the counter. Somehow it felt safer that way.

"Now," Petula began, her voice quiet and dangerous, "I don't know who among you has decided they want to cause trouble, but I'm here to tell you I've had *enough* of it."

"It's not our campaign," Wilda began, but Petula lifted her hand to silence her.

"I know it's one of you. Now, fess up, or I will disqualify *all three of you.*"

"You can't do that," Wilda said.

"Watch me," Petula snapped. "Now. Who started the fire?"

Hendry glared at Miranda, and Miranda glared right back. Wilda crossed her arms over her chest petulantly. Freddie and Gore stood stone-faced. And still, no one spoke.

"I'm *waiting*," Petula said, tapping her feet.

"I *told* you, it wasn't me," Wilda said.

"And why should we believe you?" Hendry asked.

Wilda's face went pink, and she reached into her pocket to pull out a folded letter. "Because not five minutes before the fire started, I got a letter telling me if I didn't drop out, Dag Flanigan was going to arrest me."

"Goodness, not *another* one," Hendry muttered.

Petula crossed the room and took the letter from her then brought it over to Bev. "Does this handwriting look familiar?"

Bev inspected it. "Yes, it looks similar."

"Dag Flanigan wouldn't have any reason to arrest you," Freddie said. "Not unless you have..." His eyebrows went up. "Wait..."

"Yes, you infernal boy, there would be a reason for him to do it," Wilda snapped, her pink face reddening. "I swear, I'm so tired of all this blackmail nonsense, I'm about ready to offer myself up to him. But I won't be intimidated into dropping out."

Bev furrowed her brow. "That doesn't make sense, Wilda."

"I don't care if it does," she said, settling into the chair and looking away from everyone.

Petula cleared her throat. "Well, that certainly is an admission."

"That is, of course, the third letter we received," Miranda said, clearing her throat. "My cousin received one the first day, then I received one the night of the debate." She quirked a brow at the other two. "Did either of *you* get a letter?"

Hendry gnashed her teeth. "You know I didn't."

"Hm." Miranda put her finger to her chin thoughtfully. "How strange. Mr. Silver? Did your campaign get one?"

"Yeah." Gore spoke up before Freddie could. "Got one this evening. Said if Freddie didn't drop out—"

"Wait, you did?" Freddie spun around to face his manager. "Is that the first one?"

Bev clicked her tongue suspiciously. "No, it would be the second."

Freddie shook his head. "What did it say, Gore?"

"Nothing of importance," Gore said, rubbing his chin. "Just threatening nonsense. Rabble rousing."

"Then why didn't you tell me about it?" Freddie said, his tone darkening.

"Because you didn't need to worry about it," he replied, waving Freddie off. "It was about me anyway, not…not anyone else."

"Because your brother was a kitsus," Bev said, leaning on the counter. "Right? That's why he was arrested by the queen's forces."

Gore's expression shifted. "Yeah."

"But you don't have any magic," Bev continued. "Because you were tested, and they didn't find any on you, right?"

"Right. Anyway, nothing to worry about with these letters."

"Except that you work with iron all day," Bev continued, earning a curious look from Hendry and Wilda. "So if you *did* have magic, it would've been muted. Maybe even disappeared completely. But should there be a large influx of magic, I wonder if your dormant magic would've suddenly become obvious."

Like Allen, who'd always had a bit of pobyd magic, but hadn't noticed it.

Gore's face was now ashen as he stared at Bev. "Yeah? So?"

"A kitsus is a creature with uncanny senses," Bev said. "Like the ability to see from far away. Or, in your case, *hear*."

Hendry sucked in a gasp. "It was *you*!"

"Me?" Gore laughed nervously. "I don't know what Bev's on about. Off her rocker. Spent too much time in the rosemary bread."

"Mr. Dewey," Petula said, rising slowly. "May I see the letter you say you received tonight?"

"Oh, um…" The sheen of sweat on Gore's face grew more pronounced. "I'm not really sure…don't want you to know my secret, what with Flanigan in — Hey!"

Hendry had quickly rounded the table and snatched the letter from between his fingers.

"Hm. This doesn't look like a blackmail letter. This looks like a note to Flanigan that says I'm an empath and Wilda's a barus, and we should be arrested immediately." Hendry folded up the letter and pursed her lips at Gore as Wilda went pale. "Did you pick up the wrong letter by chance?"

Gore worked his jaw, saying nothing.

Freddie, on the other hand, stared at Gore as if seeing him for the first time. "You're the one... It's been you, all this time? What in the world for?"

"You have to win, Fred," Gore said, after a moment. "You know how important it is."

"Not as important as my husband," Freddie replied, turning to him fully. "You summoned Flanigan here, too? Set the town hall on fire? What else are you hiding?"

"N-Nothing, I—"

"Well, it seems to me we've got all the questions answered," Hendry said with a cheeky grin. "Mr. Silver's campaign was the dirty one, which, frankly, is shocking to me. I thought it was the Middleburg campaign."

"But..." Wilda swallowed, looking at Gore as if she'd never seen him before. "But *how* did you know what I am? Nobody knows."

"He overheard, probably," Bev said. "There were lots of interesting conversations during the solstice, I'd wager." She turned to Gore with a scrutinizing look. "Do you still have your super hearing or has it completely gone away?"

"I don't know what you're talking about," Gore said through gritted teeth.

Everyone went still as the front door opened and Flanigan strolled in, flanked by Rustin, who was mumbling apologies to Bev and Hendry and everyone else. Flanigan surveyed the room like a predator who'd stumbled on a den full of prey, and cracked a smile.

"Well, have we had a nice discussion?" he asked. "Have we figured out which candidate was responsible for the fire? Or better yet, which candidate I should be having a chat with?"

Bev looked around. Everyone there, except Miranda and Petula, could be hauled away in irons. Freddie glared at Gore, perhaps wondering if he should sell out his campaign manager. Wilda looked like she might faint. Miranda pursed her lips distastefully. And Petula fumbled with her hands.

"I can answer that," Hendry said, standing slowly. She smiled at Freddie and Wilda, almost evilly, and turned to Flanigan. "I believe you were informed about the mess we had at the solstice, right?"

"Aye." Flanigan nodded slowly.

"Well, I have to tell you, the dark forest has been an absolute nightmare ever since," Hendry said. "It's spitting out strange little orange flowers that I'm sure are toxic. I'm honestly scared to go near them."

"I don't care about flowers," Flanigan said.

"I'm sure you think you don't, but I have a sense these might be quite illegal," Hendry said. "As for the election, other than Ms. Murtagh scheming to move our Harvest Festival with her cousin, and Mr. Dewey not having a *clue* how to run a campaign properly, there's nothing much to see. We've yet to determine who's responsible for the fire, though if you ask me, it's *probably* the Middleburg contingent." Hendry smiled at Miranda, who scowled back. "In any case, I don't think there's anything here that merits your involvement, Mr. Flanigan. But these flowers..." She shuddered. "Trust me when I say, I think you'll find them *very* interesting."

"Fine." Flanigan sniffed. "You'd better be right."

"Fabulous." Hendry looped her arm around his. "Come, come. I believe we won't be continuing the election tonight, will we, Petula?"

Petula snapped back to life. "N-no. No, I think we should postpone until tomorrow."

"Yes, give Earl a chance to look at the town hall. Make sure it's structurally sound." She nodded. "Anyway, Mr. Flanigan, I know your time is valuable. So why don't we head to the dark forest now?"

She walked with such purpose, Bev would've thought she'd been using magic on him, though the mayor was much smarter than that. And if there were orange flowers still blooming in the dark forest (though Bev was sure they were all withered), Flanigan would surely find that more interesting than the election.

When the sound of Hendry's echoing voice was gone, Wilda cleared her throat. "I think I'd like to call it a night. I'm quite...well, I'm quite tired from all this. And if we've got to do it all tomorrow, then best be ready for it."

"You aren't dropping out?" Gore said.

She glared daggers at him. "*No*. And if you want to spill my secret to Flanigan, I'll be happy to tell him yours, too. Kitsus. Goodness gracious. All this time," she muttered to herself. "Miranda. Come."

Miranda jumped, evidently shocked to be spoken to by her cousin like that, but followed her out.

Petula put her hand to her head. "I'd like to forget everything I heard this evening. Whatever magical powers everyone has…best to let them be dormant, hm?" She turned to Freddie. "Unfortunately, Mr. Silver, in light of the revelations about your campaign manager—"

"No need," Freddie said, glaring at Gore. "I'm out."

"Out?" Gore cried. "What do you mean, out?"

"I mean you took things too far, Gore," Freddie said. "And I don't care how important this thing is, it's not worth risking my husband's life." He turned to Petula. "Is there anything else you need from me?"

"N-no." Petula shook her head. "Thank you for your cooperation."

He snorted, giving a glare to Gore and a single nod to Bev before storming out the door.

"Well." Petula cleared her throat. "That's that,

then. I've got to go upstairs and lie down as well. Another long day of electioning tomorrow."

Then she was gone, leaving Bev and Gore. But before Bev could say another word to the blacksmith, he was out the door, too.

Chapter Twenty~Two

Earl came to the inn first thing in the morning to announce that while there were a few charred spots, the town hall was safe for the rescheduled election. Petula, who was enjoying one of Allen's muffins with a cup of tea, was overjoyed, as was Bev, as Petula had thought the Weary Dragon might make a suitable alternate location.

Word quickly spread that Freddie had dropped out. Though the reasons for it weren't made known, the scuttlebutt could put two and two together, and everyone was convinced it had something to do with the fire. It was somewhat amusing, at least to Bev, that the Pigsend citizenry accurately pegged the mishaps on the gruff campaign manager, and not the affable candidate. It didn't help that the blacksmith shop was closed and boarded up, either.

"Goodness, I hope Gore doesn't skip town," Ida said with a sigh as Bev put in her meat order. "Who's going to make all our ironwork? What if our wagon wheel breaks? He can't leave."

"Maybe Gilda could come back," Bev said with a shrug.

Bev was, in a word, furious at Gore for all he'd put everyone through. She still had no idea why he was so keen on Freddie becoming mayor, nor did she understand why he'd invited Flanigan to town when he, himself, could be in danger of being arrested. It didn't make sense.

There was much theorizing in the crowd as the citizens of Pigsend gathered once again to cast their votes. Now, the candidates were Hendry and Wilda, the latter of whom had found her confidence, and reclaimed her space in front of the schoolhouse. The bakers, though, hadn't provided her with more sweets, as they had other orders to fill—not to mention their jams to make. Nor did Wilda have the benefit of her cousin, who'd either declined to stay in town or was keeping a low profile.

With Freddie out of the race, there was a little more interest in Hendry, who was consoling those who'd wanted to vote for Freddie. She was in her element, shaking hands and talking to the voters as if she knew every detail about their lives. Which, as

Bev knew, Hendry *did*, thanks to that journal. But maybe it wasn't all bad. After all, if she remembered tiny Tallulah Painter's birthday and Eldred Nest's preferred instrument, it couldn't be the worst thing.

"Come to inspect the election proceedings?" Hendry asked, walking up to Bev with a smile. "Don't appear to be any more mishaps today."

"No," Bev said. "But never say never."

"A *kitsus*," Hendry muttered to herself. "I honestly can't believe I didn't connect those dots. I mean, it's not as if those creatures are quite common, but everyone knew his brother was the best person to take hunting. He could spot a field mouse from across town." She shook her head. "Suppose Gore's got the ears, then?"

Bev nodded. "Not that he's told me about it. Is he even still in Pigsend?"

"I heard him hammering away early this morning," Hendry said. "There aren't too many people who know *exactly* what he did, after all. Lots of details get lost in the mix. I'm sure given a few weeks, he'll be able to show his face without any hint of shame." She shrugged, glaring at Wilda across the square. "Worked for Wilda."

"Are you going to update your journal entry for her?" Bev asked.

"Hm. I might. I should. Serve her right. But…" She sighed. "Well, I don't put *everything* in there, you know. I have a lot more detail about *you* stored up here." She tapped her forehead.

"Yeah?" Bev snorted. "What kind of detail?"

"I think you're more than you seem, Bev," Hendry said. "But the most important detail is that I'm grateful to call you my friend."

Bev smiled at her. "I hear you want to stay on my good side."

"No, you misread that. You're supposed to stay on *my* good side." She lifted a shoulder. "Obviously."

"My mistake." Bev gazed out onto the crowd. "What did Flanigan say about the flowers? And how did *you* know about them?"

"I know about everything," Hendry said. "Flanigan's eyes nearly fell out of his head. I don't think he expected to see *those* around."

"They weren't supposed to be around," Bev said, eyeing her. "As we cultivated every last one during the solstice."

"Mm. But if someone were to grab a cutting *before* the solstice and plant it in a pot in her window, for safekeeping, then that plant might still be alive today." Hendry tapped her nose. "I always have a Plan B, Bev. Remember that."

"You aren't the one who set fire to the town hall, are you?" Bev asked, narrowing her gaze. "And we did never figure out who that rabble rouser was."

"As I told you," Hendry said with a knowing smile, "I've *read* the rules and regulations. If I was going to hire someone to cause trouble, I'd make sure it was someone registered to vote."

She walked away, and Bev started. "You didn't answer my question about the—"

"Ta-ta, Bev!"

The line to vote was once again steady, though there were fewer people voting than the day before. Petula had done her best to spread the word that people needed to vote again, as she couldn't be sure who had and who hadn't voted. But for some farmers, especially those with long days of harvesting and a longer trip into town, coming back for a second day was too much to ask.

Bev sat inside, keeping an eye out for anyone suspicious, but as the hours ticked on, and nothing happened but the slow trickle of voters, Bev found herself restless. After the sun set, and there had been no new voters for a few hours, Petula rose and walked to the front doors, gazing out into the crowd.

She turned on her heel and walked to Bev, smiling. "Well, sixty percent of the registered voters have submitted," Petula said. "Which, per my rules and regulations, means I can legally call the election now."

"What about midnight?" Bev asked.

She let out a breath. "I honestly want to go to bed so I can get on the road and leave this cursed town behind."

Bev laughed. "It really isn't that bad here. We happen to have had a spate of curiosities lately. Bad luck, that's all. You should come in the..." She rubbed her chin. "Well, there isn't really a good time to come, is there? We've had curiosities all year long, almost."

Petula sighed, wearily. "You must be tired of it."

"A little." Bev looked through the front doors, where she could see Earl and Etheldra talking with the Witzels. "But as long as I'm helping the people here, I don't really mind. Glad I can be useful."

"I'm about to close up the ballot box," Petula said, after a moment. "Unless there's another citizen who'd like to cast their vote?" She held out a blank piece of paper to Bev. "Write the name down, fold it in half, and stick it in the box. Then I'll get to counting."

Bev took it and rose slowly. Since Pip had dropped out, she hadn't really thought about who she was going to vote for, but she supposed she *should* cast a vote. If only so she could complain about whoever the mayor was. After all, if one didn't cast a vote, one didn't have room to criticize their job.

She stood at the small desk in the non-charred corner and dipped the quill in the ink. She briefly considered the two candidates, what she'd seen of them, how she'd interacted with them. What she envisioned another few years would be like with each of them.

And with a half-smile, she wrote down a name.

~

"I'm pleased to announce that the winner of the Pigsend Mayoral Election is… Jo Hendry!"

Lackluster applause met the proclamation, made at ten in the evening, and the crowd immediately dispersed, talking amongst themselves about "Who could possibly vote for Hendry?" and "Shame that Pip dropped out" and "That Hendry's got nine lives."

The mayor herself wore a satisfied smirk, but as she turned to head back to her house, Bev caught a glimpse of relief. This really had been won by the skin of her teeth, and Bev hoped Hendry would take that to heart. Perhaps ask *less* of the town innkeeper in the future, for example.

"Well, I can't say I'm too surprised by that result," Petula said. "Incumbents usually win, if only because people don't really like change. It was a little closer than I'd anticipated, though." She paused, adjusting her tunic and leaning in. "Between you, me, and the walls… I counted the votes cast yesterday, too. From a statistical standpoint, Hendry was going to lose, if that fire hadn't happened."

"Mm." Bev shook her head. "And if Freddie hadn't dropped out."

"Yes, that really tipped the scales in her favor."

Petula shook her head. "I've already forgotten why he dropped out. The pressure was too much. His campaign manager was doing unsavory things in his name." She narrowed her gaze, as if deciding between the two. "I think that first one will suffice for an explanation."

"I'm sure you don't have to stretch the truth often," Bev said.

"You'd be surprised." She chuckled. "These rural campaigns can be quite dicey, you know. Have to keep one's head on straight."

"I bet."

"Well, Ms. Bev, I do hope I can see you in the morning before I depart, but I plan to leave before the sun is up. I have a long journey to the next town. Silverkeep, I think it's called."

"Ah, say hello to their blacksmith," Bev said. "Gilda moved there from Pigsend. She was Gore's apprentice."

At Gore's name, Petula scowled. "I'll be sure to say hello from you, of course. But I'm doing my best to forget that Gore Dewey ever existed."

~

Bev wished she could forget, but unfortunately, she did have a wheel that needed replacing on her wagon. She very much wanted to delay the inevitable, but as the bakers needed their wagon for deliveries, and the Witzels did as well, there was no other option than to swallow her concern and walk into his shop. The front door was open, surprisingly, but the forges weren't on.

"Whatdy'a want?" Gore grunted from a chair in the corner.

"I've come to see about my wagon wheel," Bev said, trying to sound neutral.

"So I heard."

Bev walked up to the counter and watched him for a minute. "Did you…hear? Are you able to?"

Slowly, he nodded. "I haven't worked in a few days, so it's gotten quite loud, you know? I can hear the Brewer twins arguing about what to put in the tea blend. Earl is snoring, and Etheldra's about to smother him. Hendry's already in her office, scribbling away." He closed his eyes. "The sounds of Pigsend."

"I know you thought what you were doing was right," Bev began. "But you put a lot of people in danger."

"Those people are in danger whether I invited Flanigan or not," Gore said. "Don't you see? I did this for them. All of it is for those people."

Bev shook her head. "How do you figure?"

He rose from the chair and crossed the room. "There are plans afoot that you have no idea about. Plans to put loyal kingside people in power all over the country."

"To what end?" Bev said. "As soon as the queen's people get wind of that, they'll have you in irons."

"It's already happening. Under the queen's nose. Out here in the country, in small towns where there's no one who thinks twice. A mayor here. A magistrate there. Kingside people gaining strength and power, and getting insights into the queen's movements." He let out a breath. "Freddie was a key piece to that. But no, you had to open your big mouth."

"I didn't tell him Hans was targeted," Bev said. "He made that leap on his own."

"Hans wasn't targeted, and the only reason I gave him a letter was because of *you*," Gore said. "Vellora told me all about how you solve the mysteries. Thought if Freddie got one, you wouldn't suspect us."

"And I didn't for a while," Bev said. "You really scared Pip and Holly, though."

"I'm not going to tell anyone about PJ," Gore said. "He's a kid. Besides that, he's safe in Sheepsburg, isn't he?"

"As long as no one tells Flanigan," Bev said, pointedly.

"I swear, on this forge and my brother's life, I won't tell a soul," Gore said. "But I needed Pip out of the race, so I had to do what was necessary." He shook his head. "Should've pressed Wilda harder. Thought telling her I knew she was a barus would've worked, but she's made of stronger stuff."

"Did you hire the troublemaker too?" Bev asked. "The one who was asking all the questions? And you put Hendry's card in the question-and-answer session?"

He nodded. "The troublemaker's an old friend of Andres. In fact, the letters were Andres's idea, too. He knew Petula was coming, knew that Hendry was a shoo-in if we didn't do something about it. Got his idea from when the Witzels were blackmailed—right down to getting Flanigan involved."

Bev clicked her tongue. This was getting into matters she didn't want to know about. "Well, I'm not going to tell anyone your secret, either. Nor am I going to stop coming to you for business."

"I'd say not. Middleburg is a far way away from here." He cracked a grin, as he pulled a wheel out from the back of the shop. "Who'd replace your wagon wheels then?"

"It would be a hardship." Bev took the wheel from him. "But I have to know: are you planning on using your abilities anymore? Do I need to keep quiet or speak in an iron room?"

"If the forge is on, I can't hear a thing," he said. "And that's the truth. I prefer it that way, to be honest. Last thing I need is to hear Etheldra getting sappy with Earl—and yes, I said *Etheldra* getting sappy." He shivered. "That's enough to get me back to work for the next decade."

Bev smiled. "Good to know. Thank you for the wagon wheel." But when she tried to take it, it wouldn't budge.

"During the solstice, I overheard Andres talking with Vellora," he said, catching her gaze intently. "About you."

"Yes, we had a few conversations about my past," Bev said, pulling the wheel.

Again, it didn't budge. "Right before he left town, Andres told Vellora that he didn't want to tell you everything about your past. That he was afraid of how you'd react when you found out. But that things were coming for you that you might not be ready for, so you'd have to find out eventually."

Bev swallowed hard. When she spoke, her voice came out a whisper. "What kind of things?"

"Haven't a clue. He didn't specify." He let go of the wheel with a grin. "But all these *curiosities* happening in town, going all the way back to those soldiers causing the sinkholes… They all happened for a reason. And we're all about to find out what that reason is."

Bev continues her adventures in

Acknowlegments

As always, first thanks goes to my husband for believing in me and for managing the toddler in the evenings. Thanks, also, go to my son, for continuing to insist upon his six o'clock bedtime so I could write yet another book in the dark. Shout-out to Ms. Rachel, too. You're the real MVP.

Thanks to Chelsea, Danielle, and Lisa for being the all-star team who helps keep me going. And to my writer pals, Brett, Kelsey, and Emily, for keeping me sane.

EMPATH

Lauren Dailey is in break-up hell, but if you ask her she's doing just great. She hears a mysterious voice promising an easy escape from her problems and finds herself in a brand new world where she has the power to feel what others are feeling. Just one problem—there's a dragon in the mountains that happens to eat Empaths. And it might be the source of the mysterious voice tempting her deeper into her own darkness.

Empath is a stand-alone fantasy that is available now in eBook, Paperback, and Hardcover.

About the Author

S. Usher Evans was born and raised in Pensacola, Florida. After a decade of fighting bureaucratic battles as an IT consultant in Washington, DC, she suffered a massive quarter-life-crisis. She found fighting dragons was more fun than writing policy, so she moved back to Pensacola to write books full-time. She currently resides there with her husband and kids, and frequently can be found plotting on the beach.

Visit S. Usher Evans online at:
http://www.susherevans.com/